101 WAYS TO KILL YOUR EX-HUSBAND

BY SARAH THOMAS

To Mr. Don Bongers, a.k.a., "Mr. B", the first adult to ever read what I wrote and the first person to ever encourage me to write and to be creative. It is with enormous gratitude that I dedicate this work to you. Thank you from the bottom of my heart.

Table of Contents

Part I

Part II

Introduction

Although common sense should prevail here, common sense is rarely as common as you would like it to be. That said, I must still preface this tale with a word of caution. Any of this work resembling real events and actual persons living or dead is truly a coincidence as it is a work of fiction. It should also not have to be said that you should not kill anyone, and that this work of fiction is merely a form of entertainment for readers everywhere that need a cathartic release from many things in their lives. It is likely that any men reading this little novel may be offended, but in truth I hope that you take it to heart and understand a little more about what causes women to think and behave as they do. Women can be very forgiving and loving creatures, but they should only have to accept or tolerate so much.

I would also like to add that despite the title of this book and what takes place in its pages does not reflect any misandry (hatred of men and boys) you might think I have. I happen to love men, but I also know many women who have lived with the beasts of the human species and would prefer to live alone rather than have another mate. I myself could go either way, but I'm much more content to live alone. I also wrote this story with the intent of donating a portion of the proceeds towards charities that can help abused women escape dangerous and unhealthy relationships, if you find that more encouraging than this dark little tale.

I cannot and will not be held responsible or accountable for any rash decisions or actions readers take once they have read this book. It is for entertainment and amusement purposes only. Ergo, enjoy the story, and take heed of the underlying warnings it presents in the event that you are considering something that could drastically alter the course of your life. If you see yourself in the pages of the story, it may do well to find a healthy way to escape and recover the life you feel you have lost. The best revenge is to outlive all of those that caused you harm, and to live all your years with more joy so that they can never take or consume all that you are or all that you will become.

Love and God Speed,

Sarah Thomas

June 2021

Chapter 1: The Internal Conflict That Was More Like War

I know we've all thought about it—what if the bastard just died? What if I could just make him go away? And what the hell did I ever see in him in the first place? It's more than just a marriage gone sour, or a divorce gone really bad. It's a sense of desperation to be completely rid of someone because their ongoing presence in your life reminds you every day of what an absolutely horrible and shameful choice you made. It's funny, but my children don't remind me of him because, thank God, they don't look like the ugly bastard, but I would do away with him in a second if I could.

Wait, why can't I? Spouses knock each other off all the time, at least that is what sensational journalism and the movies and TV would have us believe. Many of them get caught, but several more wander around for decades before anyone catches them. I just had to find the right way to kill him so I would get the kids and raise them until they were old enough to look after themselves. Well, actually, until my oldest was officially an adult and my youngest could also look after herself, but her brother could be awarded guardianship.

It was nuts, *is* nuts, but I just couldn't imagine suffering another ten years with this idiot in my life. I mean, what the hell did I get a divorce for if he's still a constant pain in the ass? I swear, no matter what I did, I could not get away from Mr. Insanity, and I desperately wanted to. It was like God expected me to remember what an awful mistake I made marrying this one, and what an even more awful mistake it was to choose him as my sperm donor.

That's what he was, really—my sperm donor. Growing up in a strict Christian household it would have meant nothing but absolute shame and disgrace to get pregnant outside of wedlock. Yeah, it was the twenty-first century, but old-fashioned family ideas and ideals are not dead, and really, some of those things I still held dear. But I was twenty-eight, I heard my biological clock, not *ticking* at me, but *screaming* at me; it was about to explode if I didn't have at least one baby as soon as I could. So, I chose the first willing idiot, and now I was eternally stuck, post-divorce, with this obnoxious thorn in my side.

He had to go. He just had to go. I should have left him stay with his crazy-bitch-whore that he ran to be with down in Alabama, when he left me with a newborn and a toddler and a mountain of bills that he had long since abandoned. I so regretted asking him to come home when he realized that the "grass" wasn't greener down South than at home. I thought I had screwed up, but really, I didn't have the courage to believe I could manage on my own. He came back, turned our lives upside down again, and then left again.

Lord in heaven above, why oh why didn't I just leave him there? Why didn't he just leave the last time and stay the hell away from me and the kids? We were fine until he decided he had to pretend to be "Daddy of the Year" and return with alligator tears in his eyes for the social workers he called in to upset us, rip us apart, traumatize us and send myself and two children into a lifetime of therapy. What kind of a-hole calls CPS on the mother of his children when all she has ever done was protect them, raise them, love them, feed them, clothe them in the nicest clothes, give them lots of toys to play with, bathe and groom them, and be there for their every waking need when their father refused to be? What kind of asshole does that?

No, he absolutely had to die. One less asshole in the world makes it a slightly better place for my kids, and for me, and for anyone else who would have to put up with this piece of crap. I know my daughter won't really miss him—she'd rather not spend time with her dad, since he's made it quite clear in a nonverbal way that he wants nothing to do with her. My son would take it the hardest. The poor kid loves his dad even though he remembers every time his jackass father left. My baby boy—he has such a big heart; I just don't know if I could go through with it.

Geez, now I'm thinking I can't do this. This isn't what rational, sane people do, but this bastard has pushed me to the edge so many times I've lost count. I know I love my kids more than I hate my ex-husband, which is the only reason he isn't six feet under right now. If it weren't for my kids and the fact that I don't think they would ever forgive me if they found out, the jerk wad would be dead, or I would be as far away from him as I could possibly get.

Abuse does that to you. When you can't fight anymore, you run. You run because the legal system does not listen to you. There are no reports of physical abuse or rape, no hospital documents, nothing but your word against this beast's who puts on a good show for lawyers, judges, court officers, doctors, therapists and anybody else who's watching. He really should be given an Oscar for his performance. What a master liar.

Instead, I have mental and emotional scars. Scars from the repeated number of times he told me I wasn't allowed to speak to any other males except those in my family. That came after he read my email to an ex-boyfriend who I still talked to. I didn't see them, but I would talk to them. No harm, I thought, because I know these guys. When my girlfriends suddenly became a threat to how he expected me to behave, well, you can imagine.

When I was pregnant a second time, he could not hide his disdain. He did not want another child—he got the boy he wanted and that was enough for him. I guess we mutually used each other, but that wasn't going to stop me from having another child. When the ultrasound revealed that the baby died in utero, I was crushed. It was all he could do to contain his enthusiasm.

Then we got pregnant three months later. Our daughter was due. He was not happy. He thought I had had an affair (which I didn't—he was just psycho). Spent my entire pregnancy with her being called a whore, a slut and then he would tell me that he expected a paternity test when she was born. I almost did not allow him in the delivery room. When she was pulled from me and laid in my arms, he said, "There, now you got your girl." Like he still didn't believe it was his child or that she didn't matter to him at all. Sadly, that first rejection is still reflected in my daughter's words, thoughts and actions.

No. You know, if I can find just the right method, I won't get caught for years, and if the kids can get to adulthood, I can run after that. Yeah, that was a good plan, right? All I needed was the right way to kill him. But what method should I choose? There were dozens of ways to kill someone, and with modern technology, nothing was fool proof.

I started making mental notes, from the simplest methods to the downright craziest fantasies. In one daydream, I was a sniper who climbed up into a nearby church bell tower and shot him from three miles away. Yeah, the bastard lived less than three miles from me. It could work. If I aimed low enough on his body and used a high-tech heat sensing scope or used night binoculars that could see that far away, it would be so easy. The trajectory of the bullet from that far away would belie the position of the shooter, wouldn't it? Wait, I'm not a sniper, and it would take a really long time for me to learn how to shoot like a military expert.

Oh, well. Method number one of one hundred and one ways to kill your ex-husband is dismissed. Next.

Chapter 2: The Accidental Death

Accidental death is great, if you can pull it off and really make it look like an accident. At one point, the buffoon had asked me what I was doing for an entire week in summer. I naively thought he was going to finally take the kids on a camping trip or something to actually bond with them, or maybe make an effort to be a real dad. Stupid me.

Turns out, he wanted me to take on his weekend parenting duties for three weeks straight so *he* could go on a long vacation with his brother-in-law, fishing somewhere in the Mississippi. What an ass. I guess what angered me most about this was two-fold. One, I never got a week-long break from the children, *ever*. He only had the kids for a couple days every other weekend and our son for two nights in the middle of the week. I had them the rest of the time, and they were a handful. If it had been me asking him to take the kids for more than a week and several weekends in a row, it would have gotten ugly real fast. Either that, or he'd expect me to "return the favor" the next time he wanted a week off. It made my blood boil, and the only way to get past it was to imagine his blood boiling and his flesh on fire.

Second, he never took them anywhere. He'd have them for a few days and refused to do anything fun with them. The kids were sick of sitting around his smoke-filled, stinky apartment with nothing to do but watch TV or YouTube videos or play video games. Worst of all, our daughter was left to wander around trying to get her dad's attention in some of the worst ways possible because he would ignore her and cater to our son by playing countless hours of computer games. Yeesh, that was an unpleasant way to waste time. I felt awful every time my kids had to go over there, but I so needed a break, even for just a couple of hours.

As much as I didn't want to comply with his request, I knew if I didn't I would hear about it later. IF I had refused and asked him to take the kids for a couple of hours after the fact, he'd gaslight and get pissy and passive-aggressive until whatever plans I had were ruined before I even left the house. It was an awful way to manage parenting with someone like this, and I really didn't want to roll like that. There shouldn't have been expectations of returned favors, demands for time off from parenting, gaslighting, or other maladaptive and dysfunctional behaviors, but that's what I married and divorced, so there it was.

Then it happened. On the morning he was supposed to leave, he had a freak accident on the stairs leading up to his second story apartment. One of his feet slipped on a wet staircase and went backward through the opening behind the stairs as the rest of his body carried forward. These stairs were so steep it's a wonder he didn't fall all the way down and break his neck. I sighed at the thought about how that didn't happen, but I was silently happy that the fool broke his leg in so many places he needed pins and a cage in his leg for several weeks. Needless to say, his little vacation didn't happen.

God let me have a few seconds of retributional joy, and then slapped me with three months of headaches for reveling in someone else's pain. I spent the next several months carting the children to and from his place because the leg he broke was attached to his driving foot. Curses! Just my luck.

During this time, I could only think about the accidental ways in which someone could die, or the accidental appearances of a death. It gave me some peace in the midst of this chaos. A shove down the stairs again might be effective, but similar circumstances to those that caused his broken leg would have to be in effect. Slippery wooden stairs and a push down the long, steep flights was risking it. He might break his neck and die in a seeming accident, but he also might survive to tell someone I pushed him.

I reflected on the accidental deaths or attempted deaths in all of the cop dramas I liked to watch. Cutting someone's brake line was only effective if you knew the person was driving regularly and would be driving at a high rate of speed in the vehicle before attempting to stop. A cut brake line was obvious, unless I got lucky, and the car was completely totaled. His brother-in-law was a mechanic, and could likely to do it, which would make him a suspect. Still, it wasn't likely that I could get under his car in any way that wasn't suspicious, nor would neighbors not notice me under a car my ex wasn't currently driving.

The same thing could be said for loosening lug nuts on a tire. The tire would eventually pop off and cause an accident. Yet, he could survive that, and it might put one or both kids in danger. The factor of the children continued to overrule my vengeful fantasies.

A fire was a delightful thing to imagine as an accidental death. Fires happen all the time. He still smoked, so a smoldering cigarette tossed on his doorstep would block his only door from his apartment. He'd have to jump from a second story window if he were going to make it out alive. It would have to be set on the doorstep extremely late at night, and it would be tricky for me to sneak out that late with the kids asleep at home. It was also stupid to think I could callously leave two small kids at home in order to set their father's apartment ablaze in the middle of the night.

What if the cigarette didn't start the wood stairs on fire? What if it blew off the landing or fell through the cracks of the panels? I certainly couldn't use gasoline or some other accelerant because fire marshals could spot that in an instant. You could smell that on fire too, and if I accidentally spilled accelerant on myself, I could light myself in the fire or leave trace evidence for the police.

Then there were my ex's downstairs drug-dealing neighbors. Sure, they were scum, but they didn't deserve to be part of my wrath. The neighbors dealt drugs and raised *pit bulls* for illegal dog fights, and I had seen several suspicious characters leaving that lower apartment pocketing small items in the process. The "customers" that came and went at odd hours almost always left for a local park, where drug needles were frequently found in the grass near kids' playground equipment. As much as taking out such scum with my ex sounded like a good idea, it was the comings and goings of shady characters that would upend my plans to set the place on fire.

Accidental death by car, fire, and falling down a long way were all ruled out. Drowning wouldn't exactly work because he would have to be in a very deep area of water with no one else around to see me push and hold him under, or to cause him to drown. He wasn't a great swimmer, but people will fight you to their last when held under water. That much I was very aware from the times I had to bathe Alzheimer's patients and they would slap, punch, kick, and scratch you to pieces just for putting them under the running shower. Furthermore, it would mean that we would have to be somewhere in water as a "family unit". My kids could see everything, and I would be forced to play the part of a friendly ex-wife. The thought of doing anything to create an accident scene that would require me to get that close or show enough skin to get close made me sick.

Hot water burns were accidental, and the thought of boiling his flesh to tons of painful blisters was entertaining, but again too gross. He would have to be boiled internally too in order to die, and that was just not going to happen. I didn't have a giant microwave to blast his goose with microwaves for several minutes to make that work, nor did I have a giant cannibal cauldron that he would accidentally enter or tip for that to happen. It was fun to imagine it though, right up the point where the scalded flesh peeled away, or the giant microwave made him explode. Yes, definitely too gross and too messy.

Then it occurred to me that other accidental deaths could include being hit by a car, such as I accidentally hit him and claim I couldn't see him. Unfortunately, there was no scenario that didn't first place me in a predicament that would somehow put him in front of or behind my car, even if he did chase after my vehicle or was helping me out of snow or mud.

Death by plane was also unlikely, and although railroad tracks riddled the towns in which we lived, it would be difficult to time the trains that passed through and manage to get him to go for a walk near the tracks at just the right time to shove him in front of an oncoming train. It would also have to be at night because train engineers would see me shove him during the day. He certainly wasn't a believable hobo, so knocking him out and tying him to the tracks for the train to finish him later wouldn't work either.

Accidental death by drug overdose was probably the last one to hit me. As far as I know, he had never done any drugs that were lethal enough, although he had admitted to taking his niece's ADHD medicine and staying awake for more than three days. I know he also popped some of our son's ADHD pills when it suited him, and there was the downstairs neighbor that was definitely selling drugs. I don't know of anyone else on food stamps and welfare that drive Cadillacs and sports cars and have a boat that aren't into some sort of nefarious money-making scheme. The trouble was, he wasn't likely to overdose on anything anytime soon, and it would be very difficult to make it look like an overdose.

However, this last accidental option wasn't totally scrapped. It struck me that if I really put my mind to it, I might make it look good. It would take a lot of careful planning, and a lot of perfect timing. I put it on the back burner for another day when he resumed taking the kids by picking them up himself and not expecting me to do all the driving.

Chapter 3: Poisons, Toxins and Venom

Poison. Yeah, poison is great. Unfortunately, any purchase of poison would send red flags to the police when they came to investigate. What about exotic poisons? Home-distilled poisons? I started to do some research. There were a lot of natural poisons in the world and man-made poisons too. The trouble was, you had to get close enough to him to get the poison on him or in him. Ew.

He was such a toxic being. I used to muse about the fact that he was so toxic it was a wonder that no one close to him was dead by proximity. He was able to take any situation, lie his ass off, and make you feel like it was your fault, and that you were the one that was crazy. Finding myself in such a toxic relationship as that is often what led me to think about poisons, toxins, and venom.

I can remember early on our marriage thinking about ways to kill him. Yup, hated him even then. I had to convince myself that marriage would change him because I felt like I couldn't back out of marriage when we were mere weeks to the day. I knew he was wrong; I felt it in my gut and had experienced some of his ugly nature before ever reaching the alter.

I hated what I was tied to, what I was forced to endure. I just waited, thought, planned, plotted, and waited some more. All the horrible things...I wanted to let them go, but every time when I was ready to let go, the asshole would do something really awful again, and everything from the past would resurface. When I would bring these things up, he'd just tell me I was the psychotic one, I was the one that made it all up. Sure, the emotional pain I feel isn't real, the trauma isn't real, it's all in my head, that never happened, blah, blah, blah. My therapists (I had several over the years because all of them couldn't believe I was still in this vicious cycle with him, and they would quit being my therapists) had to keep reaffirming reality for me because I wasn't sure what reality was after some time of living with him.

I had to use other people as sounding boards to help reaffirm that these things happened too. I had to be sure that what he said and did wasn't normal by any means, and that I was right to question it all. I was trying desperately to make sure I didn't make anything up, because only he and I were ever in the room when he would verbally assault me. I would have gladly accepted the fact that none of it was real, but not at the expense of him projecting his own insanity onto me. Nope. At one point I had decided to secretly begin recording our conversations so that I could play them back for therapists and other people in my life. Their jaws just dropped, and it wasn't even some of the worst things he ever said to me. I dropped the ball on recording him whenever he flipped into his on/off screaming fits. Recording the worst of it really would have helped me later on, but I didn't know that, and I was too stunned and terrified to secretly record those moments. That is why I began looking at ways to remove this monster from my life.

Back then, he smoked heavily. Back then, injecting poison or toxins into his cigarettes would have been so easy, because the cigarettes probably contained many of the same poisons and toxins that the American Cancer Society listed on their site as ingredients in cigarettes. Sure, he was already poisoning himself, but what if I helped it along? Everyone knows that cigarettes are a very long, slow way to die. Even then, it's not as though it's a guaranteed death either. Hell, look at George Burns. That comedian smoked cigars well into his nineties and never croaked. Damn, there was no way I was going to wait that long for the cancer sticks to kill him.

What poison would it be? Accidental overdoses in his cigarettes of just the right poison could help. Arsenic? Formaldehyde? Rat poison? Arsenic would be too quick, and too obvious in the blood stream. Enough of that injected into his cigarettes would cause an instant heart attack.

That might be believable though. He had extremely high cholesterol and really high blood pressure. Passing out in a heart attack after smoking a cigarette or two with arsenic would work. Then again, the coroner would check the blood and look for anything out of the ordinary. Higher than usual amounts of arsenic, even if they were present in the rest of his pack of smokes, would be too close to home for the cops and investigators. They would know.

Then there was our infant son at the time. Second-hand smoke kills, but surely second-hand smoke laced with extra arsenic…what if the second-hand smoke with extra arsenic killed my baby boy too? I'd want to die myself. That also meant that rat poison was out.

What about formaldehyde? That was actually a preservative of the body after death. Over time, a little extra of that each day would pickle him from the inside out. He'd eventually begin to feel short of breath, stiff, and light-headed. After some time, he'd start to be vacant, vapid, and speechless. The trouble is, he would have to be rushed to the hospital after he came close to death so that I could remove all speculation and blame from myself. What if they restored him and wanted to do more tests? That would not work.

If I waited outside the apartment then, went somewhere, anywhere for a day or two and took the baby with, then it could work. Maybe. I'd have to be sure the end was near. Then plan to leave. Then the waiting game would start. Who would believe that I would leave a sick spouse to go off traipsing with a baby and come back later to a dead spouse? Would anyone actually believe that?

Even if I got past all of that, what about the coroner? It is not as though I had money to buy off the coroner or claim that we were devout Jews that would not allow an autopsy. I would have to get the corpse from the house to the funeral home and get the body full of formaldehyde. Once the body was filled with the death preservative, it would be impossible to tell that asswipe was bumped off. But that was a truly impossible feat.

I waited and watched and thought and researched. What else could I do? Of course, there was always his Cola. He drank four liters of the sick, syrupy stuff a day. That could hide the taste of any poison. Hell, you could probably put anti-freeze in his Cola, and that would do it. The only problem is getting enough poison into the bottle to kill him, and not too much to be suspicious. So, how much anti-freeze can kill a person? Apparently, for an adult, diluting a quarter cup of the stuff in a two-liter bottle of Cola is sufficient. There was just one problem with that. What if he did not drink it all at once? What if he saved some and his liver filtered out the poison before it had enough of an effect? What if he went to the hospital for the effects he was feeling, and they pumped his stomach? Worst of all, what if he served some Cola to a visiting buddy? Ugh. Too many "what-ifs."

Yet, I was reminded of all the ways he was such a toxic person himself. He constantly fought and argued the dumbest things. He always thought he was right, even though he could be led around by the nose by thoughts and ideas that were so incredibly *wrong*. He didn't really think for himself but chose to believe what "those in authority" told him to believe, and then made every attempt to push those ideas onto me and the children. I was trying to teach the children to question *everything* and to think critically and analytically for themselves, something my ex never did and refused to do because his sources were right, which made him right and me wrong. That's a very trying and difficult thing to do when your children already have developmental deficits in cognition and then a toxic parent constantly screws with their brains.

It's one hell of an existence when you blindly accept what a government tells you rather than to think for yourself. It's even worse when you even accept what movie critics tell you about different movies and treat their opinions as hard-set doctrine and do not formulate your own opinions on even the least of these subjects. Worst of all were the constant arguments that these stupid things led to, making the toxic effects on our marriage and our post-divorce life unbearable.

What makes a toxic person so toxic? I had some idea, having lived through it and still having to deal with the behaviors on an infrequent basis. I faced rage, I faced threat of physical harm, I faced isolation away from friends and family, either forced or coerced into hiding by the toxic individual or because friends and family couldn't deal with the constant drama that surrounded me. They abandoned me because of the toxicity of this person in my life. It's as though the toxic person swallowed a ton of poison at some point in their lives or inhaled toxic fumes and it just screwed with their brains and their personalities.

The truth is a lot scarier. The truth is that toxic people aren't really born; they're made. They may have contributing mental health issues like my ex, but they grew up in home environments that were twisted and evil. They take that out on everyone they have a relationship with, spewing forth the acidic unpleasantness they have lived with all their lives in order to incur equal pain and suffering with others in the hopes that making others miserable somehow makes them less lonely, more powerful, or less miserable in the process. It's an ugly cycle that stops when a healthier, smarter person puts an end to it, and that is exactly why I was considering poisons and toxins to end the cycle and end the life of a toxic individual.

Okay, now I'm considering some of the more common poisons. Of course, they would work. Poisons always work if you know how to give them and know how high of a dose you need. Could I get him to actually *eat* or *drink* the poisons? That might be very tricky. We've been divorced for almost a decade, and I think those opportunities are almost past us.

If I could get him to drink some poisons, I would have to put it in the only drinks he consumes. Cola could even disguise the taste of some poisons. Beer would too, but he might be far more suspicious of me offering him a beer because I don't drink beer. He might take a free bottle of Cola from me, but how would I get the poison into it? What poison would I use?

Clearly, I could not open the bottle because he might see that and ask why I'm giving him an open bottle of Cola. My fingerprints would be all over that, too. That would be the dumbest way to do it.

I could use a diabetic needle to inject poison into the bottle. That could work. The diabetic needle is small enough that it would not make a noticeable hole. That gave me an idea. Could I get my hands on some insulin? Could I poison him with an overdose of insulin in his sugar-laden soft drink of choice? Maybe. It would have to be a lot of insulin, given that the corn syrup and sugar in his favorite beverage could counteract that.

Ugh. There was still the remote chance he would share the soda pop with someone else. Then there was the fact that the bottle would have to be disposed of before the police found it. The bottle injected with anything from Warfarin diluted from rat poison to a double dose of nitroglycerin tablets for heart attack patients could work. It would look like he took too much of his own medication. Yet, there was always that chance that the kids would get to the bottled beverage before he did.

Okay, scratch that-at least for now. What other poisons could work? A transfer poison? This is a poison that transfers from the poisoner to the victim. I always loved how female spies used poison lipstick to pull this off. They didn't even have to kiss mouth-to-mouth. A kiss on the cheek was sufficient.

What poisons are transferred trans-dermally? Better question: how could I touch him to kill him? That thought alone was nauseating. It was also dangerous, because, again, the children. I did not want to touch them before transferring enough poison *to him*. As it turns out, transdermal poisoning could only be effective if I could slap a medicine patch or a tainted smiley-face sticker on him and keep it in place for at least twenty minutes. That was out.

What about a stinger poison? Dozens of TV shows over the years showed rings and walking canes with hidden "stingers" to poke poison into a body. The trouble with rings is that I could accidentally stick myself, and then I would need an antidote. The cane with the secret "stinger" could work, but to get close enough, I would have to disguise it another way. I wasn't the type to go walking about with a cane!

The concept was a spring-loaded lancet dipped in a powerful poison. I didn't know if I was clever enough to figure that out. In what normal-looking object could I hide a poison-laden lancet to spring on the bastard at just the right moment in a way that did not seem out of place? Geez, this was hard.

Switching gears, I have to think about the poison. It has to be something strong enough and lethal enough that just poking him once with the device would do the trick. I remembered a Russian spy story from years ago where the spy was poisoned but it took the police *weeks* to find out how the poison was transmitted and exactly what the poison was. Weeks might give me enough time to find a non-extradition country and fly there, never to return.

What was the poison? Apparently, it was *polonium*. Holy cow, this stuff was lethal. You only need less than a single tiny drop injected into a person's bloodstream to kill your target. No wonder the assassin was so successful in his mission against an experienced Russian spy. The spy didn't have a chance.

Along those same lines there were other really lethal substances. Jellyfish toxin and rattlesnake venom were too exotic. The lazy lump never left his house for anything, so it would be really suspicious to the police and far too easy to discover by mass spectrometry and a forensic toxicologist if I used snake or jellyfish venom. I didn't know enough about pufferfish venom to extract it from a pufferfish to make that work either. Besides, no one would believe he ate poisoned fugu unless he actually ate some fugu, which was highly unlikely.

You can milk the venom from animals and squeeze toxins from others. It is particularly dangerous, and those that do so regularly have to wear a lot of special equipment to protect themselves from the stings, bites, toxins and venom. For example, I could buy a pet rattlesnake. I wasn't into the idea of buying a pet rattlesnake really, since such "exotic" pets were hard to come by and much more expensive to care for. Yet, once you got the hang of milking a rattlesnake's fangs for venom it wasn't so bad. Similarly, you could "milk" a live scorpion's tail, wasp or bee stingers (although bees would die instantly after a single milking), "milk" the fangs of a black widow or brown recluse spider, or any other venomous creature. I shied away from most of those animals, arachnids and insects just because I found them far too creepy to handle and I was too afraid they would get loose in the house.

Using spider venom directly could work. Where we lived there were enough brown recluse spiders. The problem was safely catching one, and then trying to place the spider directly on him. I could turn the spider loose in his house somehow, but then it could kill the children when they were visiting, or the cat he kept there. No, I just wanted HIM dead, and no one else. I stuck the spider idea on the back burner though, because it was believable as an accidental death.

Another lethal poison was anthrax. While we were married, a rash of envelopes were delivered to people containing an unassuming white powder. Within minutes of opening the envelopes and touching or inhaling the powder, these people were convulsing and dying. That was quite the image in my brain; the bastard rolling around on the floor, with foam exiting his mouth, and his eyes rolling back in his head. It was a little too gruesome for me, really, but it was a moment of pleasantness when I imagined how much he would suffer. He deserved to suffer. I had to find a poison that would make him suffer like that, but not be as gruesome. The anthrax was too dangerous to everyone else, too, and I would have to mail it, which would directly draw the police back to me. Well, that was a definite "no."

Another poison delivered by mail at that same time was ricin. It was a powder extracted from the common castor oil plant. It required one milligram per kilogram of human body weight to be lethal. That meant extracting enough home-grown ricin to annihilate an 80-kg male. In a 1:1 ratio of ricin milligrams to kilograms of body weight, I'd have to get no less than 80 kg of ricin from castor oil buds and I would have to do everything possible not to inhale any myself in the process. How would I get that into him without him knowing? The only real answer lay in placing the ricin in vegetable oil for cooking, but traces would be left behind in and on everything the ricin-laced cooking oil touched. Food cooked in this tainted mixture would make anyone very sick, and I would have to make a very large batch of ricin to get enough of it into his system to kill him. Anyone else sharing a meal with him would be dead too, which means it was one of the least possible methods of death.

Packages delivered through the mail with ricin bombs inside were clever enough, but it had to be crafted perfectly. There could be no room for errors, and it could not blow up in anyone else's face except the recipient. Ricin as a dry powder was faster acting than it would be suspended in a liquid, but unfortunately, I did not have enough skill to build such a deadly package. I also wanted to be absolutely certain the ricin bomb package only blew up on *him*, and it was quite out of my control once the package was in the mail or on a table at his place.

Natural plant-derived poisons also came to mind. Socrates committed suicide under duress by drinking hemlock. What a classic way to die, although it was almost too good for *him* (i.e., the ex, not Socrates). You could die by ingesting the tiniest part of this plant, and in the spring right before hemlock produces flowers is when it is most lethal. Then, all you have to do is touch it with a bare hand and you are done. Drinking a "tea" made from its leaves is what did Socrates in, but he did not even need that much to kill him. The trouble was, it was hard to get. It would have to be grown someplace safe and out of the way where no one else could touch it or find it. I would have to wear a protective HAZMAT suit just to cultivate it. Yeesh, that was way too much work for a death that would not be immediate. Respiratory failure by hemlock sounded great, but thirty minutes to wait for him to die was too long. He could easily call an ambulance before he felt the full effect of the poison.

What about deadly nightshade? Who would not want to die of such a beautifully named plant? Its other name, *belladonna*, sounds equally beautiful. The problem here was that I would have to somehow get the seeds or leaves, crush them up, and find a way to get you-know-who to consume them. The risks were huge because anything that was edible would easily be passed to a child and within reach if a kid was hungry and found the food in my ex's fridge or cupboard. He really did not eat cake, pie, brownies, or other baked sweets, so it is not as though that would work out with any poison I could find. I could get really "crafty" and buy a pack of his cigarettes, his preferred brand, slice open a cigarette down the length of it, mix tobacco with the nightshade, and then re-roll and seal up the cigarette. He really would not know what hit him, considering that the nightshade causes lovely hallucinations right before it kills you.

Yet, how much nightshade would it take? Portion control was such a problem where poisons were concerned. You would think that something like poison would be an easy way to kill someone, but I was discovering that it was definitely a fine art and a science all rolled into one. During the Renaissance, women used the derivative of the belladonna plant to dilate their pupils. Optometrists were still doing this, but only to get a closer look at one's retinas. To use it as both a poison and an eye drop would require a lot of careful planning and skill, but I chalked it up to a possibility just because I liked the sound of it.

Then I came across wolfsbane in a movie. It struck my interest. Witches used wolfsbane, but so did natural healers. Turns out, wolfsbane can do both; heal and kill. It is such a pretty and unusual flowering plant, too. It kind of looks like an iris, but without the bearding and other colors. It contains a chemical that lowers one's blood pressure.

Jackass had high blood pressure. What if I got him to ingest wolfsbane somehow? Would it kill him, or just make his blood pressure perfect? I imagined him slowing down, feeling relaxed, having his blood pressure lower and lower until it did not exist. He would just convulse after a while, and that would be it. Still, how would it interact with the medication he already took for hypertension? Would it speed up the death and make it really obvious? If it did that, it would be really suspicious looking. On the other hand, it could just slowly lower his blood pressure down to nothing, and it might be enough to look like a cardiac arrhythmia gone wrong. Since wolfsbane is sold in natural foods and supplement stores, I could just plant a bottle of it in his apartment and maybe that would be enough. Hmmm…. I liked it, but I wanted something more painful.

I had access as a nurse to dozens of medications that could interact with his medical conditions or with the medications he was already taking. Slipping a few pills of the wrong kind of medication into his pill bottles wasn't too difficult when we were married, but I would have quickly been the first suspect. Now that we were divorced, getting those pills that would either counteract or have a dangerous interaction with his regular pills would be even more difficult. I would have to locate his pills in his medicine cabinet and find out what those pills looked like before selecting pills that could be mistaken for what he already took. The other sticking point was that he'd have to take all of the pills I planted, or it would be too simple for the police to figure out where he got those odd pills from.

I was fascinated by the fact that there were hundreds of poisonous flowers and plants. Trying to unravel and sort through them all was astounding. Many were quite common, like irises, hyacinths, and European holly. Others were woodland plants that may only grow in certain regions or greenhouses in the world. The Medici's of Italy and the poisoned garden of the Duchess of Northumberland are two examples of gardens grown with the specific intent of proliferating the world's most poisonous plants. I found this quite intriguing, especially in light of the English laurel bush, whose brush clippings give off toxic and invisible fumes in an enclosed space. The clippings cause the person inhaling the fumes to fall asleep, and then die when oxygen levels are not restored in the enclosed space. A nice "arrangement" of flowers and toxic laurel brush on his kitchen table may kill him, but not if I couldn't quash ventilation of any kind. At most, it might just make him really sleepy and give him a headache unless I could shut off the apartment's vents and lock up windows and doors. It also meant that I would have to be present, and I would have to wear a contractor's ventilator mask to avoid being poisoned as well.

Of course, it did occur to me to make it look like I too had been slightly poisoned but had left before the poison could have any real effect on me. It was a major risk to be sure, and I didn't want that kind of risk without reassurance.

If I combined laurel cuttings with a flowering plant called Angel's trumpet, it would ensure death in just minutes. Angel's trumpet grows in South America, which made it hard to get in North America. However, a small amount of pollen from its flowers created both an aphrodisiac and a hallucinogenic effect. He would slowly drift into a sleepy state from the laurel cuttings and then die from too much of the Angel's trumpet. That would make quite the centerpiece on his kitchen table, but I would have to remove it after confirming he was dead. I would have to cover the arrangement with a garbage bag and handle it all with gloves and a protective set of clothing to dispose of the brush and flowers and not die myself. Maybe what I needed to do was give him laurel cuttings with pussy willows, which would look very innocent, and once he fell under the sleeping spell of the laurel, introduce the pollen of the Angel's trumpet into his nose or mouth. A big problem was the trace evidence here, which could be discovered easily in the coroner's office. I also didn't like the idea that he would just sweetly and peacefully pass away. He deserved much worse than that.

There was one constant issue with all of the animal toxins and the plant poisons, though, and that was ingestion, inhalation, or transference. I just did not know how to get something close enough to him to introduce a poison or toxin into his bloodstream, and there was far too much risk in getting him to drink, smoke, inhale, or ingest something. Injecting him with a syringe of venom wasn't exactly simple either. Everything had to be perfectly planned, and he would have to trust me completely again, which meant being really nice to him for an exceptionally long time.

I nearly barfed thinking about that last part. I switched gears to think about methods with more malice. That helped ease the queasiness in my gut.

Chapter 4: Sharp Instruments for a More Painful Revenge

A quote from a Shakespeare play talks about "the unkindest cut." It references how Brutus inserted himself into the massacre of his long-time friend, Julius Caesar. It was Brutus who first stabbed Caesar to end Caesar's life, and it was Brutus who continued to stab his friend to make sure the ruler and friend was dead.

I have often reflected on that, given that words can cut as deeply as any sharp knife, and actions that leave a person to be fearful and wanting to escape someone others are supposed to love and trust are equally as awful. Living with someone who constantly wants to cut you down with words, berate you, belittle you, denigrate and degrade you to control you and make you submit to their will is no way to live. The "unkindest cut" to me was all of the ugly things I had to hear on a nearly daily basis with my husband and then ex-husband.

"You're too fat and lazy," after he insisted that only chubby women aroused him, and the house was made a mess by himself and children while I was working double shifts to support him and the kids.

"You suck at parenting. You're an awful mother and don't deserve to have children," for years after the kids were born despite the fact that I was the parent who always stayed with them and helped them with everything.

"You're a slut and a whore, and that child isn't mine," after I became pregnant the third time and never once had an affair while he had frequent affairs.

"I no longer find you attractive and I'm not in love with you anymore," after he ran off to be with someone he had never seen before and had only met through an online video game.

"You're a selfish bitch," after I had just worked several double shifts and refused to give him every dime of overtime I made so that he could spend it on some new toy for himself.

If there was an ugly statement that could be said and could be used to cut my heart and soul to the quick, he used it. Whenever I could, I had to find a quiet, isolated place to sit and cry to avoid being verbally sliced to ribbons just for crying. I had a right to cry; the unkindest cut were words that told me I had no reason to cry like a baby after being told the ugliest things and being "informed" that these were truths and I should "suck it up and accept these truths."

They were not truths, and I knew it, but the pain of the words as sharp instruments made me want to reach for a sharp instrument to hurt him back. I supposed it probably wouldn't have much effect, considering he was a cutter and burned himself with cigarette butts, but I still wanted to hurt him with something sharp, the same way his words had hurt me. I was also fearful that at some point he would turn the cigarette butts and razor blades on me, or worse, the children.

I must admit; I have had my share of fantasies involving sharp instruments for exacting revenge. There are so many points on the human body where a slice or a stab would cause blood loss and death in a matter of minutes. By the time he could call an ambulance and wait for it to arrive, they could not possibly save him. If you know exactly where to strike, and how deep to go, lethality is imminent.

That is why I switched from poisons and toxins to the idea of something sharp and oh, so painful. Messy, to be sure, but almost always effective. I personally liked anything really barbaric or deadly; it was already a hobby of mine. When Medieval shows featured battles with period weapons and torture chambers, you can bet I wanted to check those out. Those people definitely knew how to annihilate the human body in ways that make most people cringe. I had to admire that, even though some things, like a chastity belt, made me want to walk cross-legged back out of the showroom door.

My nursing background and my studies in biology, anatomy, and physiology made it possible for me to know where to strike someone with something sharp so that the target would bleed to death in minutes. I pictured shoving a sharp, rusted instrument into the femoral artery of the demon himself, and watching as he stumbled, bled, tried to reach his phone, but could not.

Even if he could reach his phone on time, it would take an ambulance four minutes to come from the hospital to his sad apartment, and he'd be dead before they could get him onto a gurney and get an IV in his arm.

If I didn't go for the femoral artery, there was always the brachial artery, the carotid artery, and the thoracic and abdominal arteries that ran through the trunk of the body into the pelvis to branch off into the legs. Besides, you would have to stab deep through the front center part of the body or through the back center past the spine to get to the two main arteries in the trunk of the body.

In consideration of all the places you could stab or cut a person to make them bleed out, there was still the consideration of the weapon. Butcher knife or kitchen knife was just too "horror movie" cliché. A machete was most effective, but I would have to buy a machete and then use it to hack a lot of stuff down to make a reasonable excuse/alibi for having it in the first place.

I liked swords. Nay, I should say I *loved* swords. I had quite the collection of reproductions, but they were usable reproductions. Their blades had been sharpened prior to selling them to consumers. The katana, the Civil War infantry sword, the claymore, the two-fisted broadsword of a barbarian, and the Medieval sword of a Spanish knight were all in my collection. Ninja swords and short stubby Roman blades were in my collection too. It would be so easy to pick one of these and use it to just end him. I decided against something I already owned because a) it would be too obvious and too convenient a choice, and b) it would not be easy to clean blood and tissue off of something I wanted to keep without risking the police finding it and analyzing it for evidence.

I didn't own any daggers. I liked kris blades, but daggers were too much like knives. It would be easy for a forensics pathologist to look at the wound or wounds, take measurements of their depth and pattern, and the width of entry to exit of the blade and know right away what kind of dagger it was. Since a kris's wavy blade was unique to its design, that would be a dead giveaway for the investigating officers.

Other sharp instruments of pain infliction and death would require a lot more force to use. As much as I reveled in the daydream of smashing in his skull with a mace and all of its fierce-looking spikes, that would be too obvious. Too many holes in the skull of equal size, width, and length would give away what the smashing sharp weapon was.

Then I considered needles. Needles creep everyone out, and for good reason. You can insert these sharp objects almost anywhere in the human body to incur enormous pain. Even an acupuncture needle accidentally inserted in the wrong place would cause pain rather than a release from pain. I could see him, with his back turned to me, and I sneaking up to stab him with an acupuncture needle right into his back or neck where it would cause him the most pain and the most damage. A needle to kill the nerve signals to the heart, or the diaphragm, or even to the lungs would suffice. The question was, how would I get my hands on an acupuncture needle? If I somehow managed that, how would I get close enough to the wretched bastard to stab him with the needle where it counts? I certainly was not a licensed acupuncturist, so how would I know exactly where to insert that needle for the desired effect of extreme pain, paralysis of vital organs, and ultimately, death?

I reminded myself that there were other ways to die by needle. Injecting poisons was one, but I wanted the death to look like an accident, a suicide, or a stupid mistake. I liked the idea of a suicide, since he had already tried to commit suicide once before after our daughter was born. However, he would never do anything to inject himself with a poison.

Injecting something more natural might be a possibility. Injection of insulin was great, but I did not know anyone who would give me enough insulin to create a lethal injectable dose of the stuff. He was not diabetic yet, either so injections using needles and insulin were out.

Certain vitamins that one could inject, like potassium, was a possibility. If you inject an incredible amount of potassium into the blood, it shuts down organs. You need a certain amount of potassium each day, but too much will kill you. Vitamin K was another possibility. It is used to help blood clot, and I could just see his blood turning into a thick sludge in is vascular system and killing him in seconds. I heard it was really a painful way to go, too, and that was something I liked about it.

Of course, I could just inject him with air. A single air bubble inside a syringe is lethal enough to cause a heart attack. It is why nurses make sure there are no air bubbles inside an IV drip line, and that needles that draw liquid injectable medications always and only draw it from inverted vials. They want to avoid accidentally drawing an air bubble into the syringe, which would then be accidentally injected into the patient. The best part of "death by air bubble" or death by Vitamin K or potassium was that they were all completely untraceable after death. That definitely drew me closer to this idea than any others I had shelved as possibilities.

Chapter 5: Strangulation

There has to be hundreds, possibly thousands, of women out there who picture strangulating their husbands or ex-husbands or boyfriends at least once. Maybe they picture it for sexual pleasure, or maybe they picture it because the guys in their lives have just done something utterly stupid and frustrating. Maybe they picture it as a means of emotional release from the extreme tensions in their relationships. All I know is that strangulating my ex was something I envisioned *a lot*.

He constantly did dumb, foolish, stupid and selfish things. For example, there was the time when he ran payday errands. He was literally next door to our bank, and instead of just driving up to the bank or heading into the front door to the ATM, he went to the ATM at the gas station next to the bank. This ATM charged us $5 to withdraw our money, and then our bank charged us some more money for using an out-of-bank ATM. So, so, dumb. When confronted he first gave the excuse of "Well, the bank was closed." When told that the ATM was right there and that the door was always open, he realized he had been caught, and tried to laugh it off. Thanks, because you know I just enjoy working an entire hour of my life to pay ATM and bank fees for stupidity.

Then there was the time he refused to wake up to watch our son when I had to go to class at the local university. I had forgotten a book in our apartment just as I got into the car. I went back into the house and our son wasn't on the bed next to his father. When I in a panic had awakened him and asked where our baby boy was, he foolishly said, "right next to me" even though it was clear our son wasn't there. I found our son sitting on the floor, playing with a sharp scissors and about twenty seconds away from inserting the tip of the scissors into the wall outlet. If I hadn't come back for my textbook, I would have come home to find our infant son dead.

My personal favorite stupid moment of all time was when I left to go to the grocery store and left our son in his father's care again. I came home to find our son in just his diaper standing on the front porch of our house in the middle of a frozen February day. Our son could have suffered frostbite, hypothermia, or worse, been snatched off the front porch right there. Where was his dad? Asleep in bed.

So many times, so many examples of when I really wanted to strangle my husband and then strangle my ex-husband. So many terrifying, awful, unforgettable, and even unforgivable moments led me back to visions of strangulation. Funny, then, what happened the month after our daughter was born.

At that time, I had kicked him out and forced him to take stock. Things had gone really bad, and I had enough. He was so emotionally unstable, and I was exhausted from the gaslighting and exhausted from being made to feel like I was crazy and not the other way around.

I falsely assumed that "if he really loves us and wants to make this work, he will finally accept psychological help and counseling." Terrible mistake, that. You can't make anyone accept a negative view of themselves, accept responsibility, or accept that they have some work in their personal self that needs doing.

He eventually ended up living in his sister's basement. He was miserable, and he had left about 90% of his belongings in the last apartment so he could run away from more responsibilities (i.e., paying overdue rent). He was undoubtedly depressed but considering that he had admitted to suffering from depression when we met, it wasn't all that surprising that a change of events in his life led him to a deeper depression. I just didn't know how deep or how dark.

This night in particular, he was visiting. I had put our son to bed, and our newborn daughter was curled up on my chest fast asleep; so sweet, so innocent. He was attempting to make an argument to come home and move back in. I wasn't having it, and to avoid waking our daughter I put her in her bassinet in the next room.

I felt like something was really off about him. Something in the air was charged in a weird way. I was very uncomfortable with how he was acting. It was wrong, and my motherly instincts kicked in. We argued more about him getting some counseling, and not moving back in until he was serious about making changes. He refused, stormed out and walked back to his sister's. I was petrified, so I locked the windows and the doors.

A few hours later, the phone rang. His sister was freaking out. I wasn't coming over there in the middle of the night with a newborn and a toddler out of bed to resolve whatever manic episode he was having, and told her so. Told her to call crisis or the cops or whatever. I tried to go back to bed. Twenty minutes later, she called saying he tried to hang himself. I knew he was whackadoo, but that was really something.

At that moment, I sort of felt bad, but then I bolstered my feelings of knowing that if I had let him stay that night, he might have killed all of us. We dodged a bullet, but unfortunately the proverbial shooter survived. I was still stuck in this endless loop of madness.

For years after this, I would imagine strangling him with ropes, tying him up with a noose and kicking the chair loose with a typed note pinned to his shirt, or using my bare hands when I was in a fit of absolute anger with him. The trouble with using strangulation as your method of killing someone, however, is that it is too easy for police to determine the cause of death. Fingerprints and handprints and strangulation marks become bruises that can be matched to your own hands and fingers. Any sort of ligature leaves its own set of marks. Attempting to hide the marks by using something soft like a pillow makes it that much harder to strangle a person to death. Then there's the fact that actually strangling someone instead of apparent suicide by hanging shows up in the way the hyoid bone breaks.

For those that don't know, the hyoid bone is this tiny bone at the top of your windpipe. It is suspended in your neck by a couple muscles and ligaments. The natural tendency of someone doing the strangling is to place thumbs or ligatures right over this area and squeeze, thereby breaking the bone when the victim tries to break free. A forensic pathologist knows the difference between a broken hyoid bone by ligature and a broken hyoid bone by force of one's hands. It also takes incredible upper body strength to strangle a full-grown man, making this the most complicated way for any woman to attempt to kill her ex-husband.

He would have to be completely sedated, unconscious, and tied down tight to avoid fighting off the ex-wife trying to kill him…I didn't see myself being able to pull all that off because it required the perfect storm of circumstances to manage. Hanging by a noose was only possible if he was already unconscious, and if I had strong rope and the perfect beam to hang him from. Still, I would have to hold his body up or hoist it up on my own, and that just seemed too much like work. I would just have to imagine such an ending when I needed an emotional release, and then let the actual action go. I also didn't want the kids to accidentally witness their father hanging by a rope; that's too much trauma on top of trauma for them.

\

Chapter 6: Firearms and Drive-By Shootings

It's a kill or be killed kind of world. If you believe in the theory of evolution, you know that survival of the fittest demands that you kill to survive or succumb to being killed yourself. If you believe in creationism, then you know that people have an inherently destructive streak that causes many to kill others, and only the best self-defense against being killed is to kill, or at least, knock your assailant out cold and then run far, far away.

It's the kind of thing you think about when your mind wanders and you're daydreaming about all the people that really tick you off. A sane person manages control over him- or herself by refraining from killing those who really make it difficult to survive in this world. It's the insane person that "goes postal" and takes a gun into work and just points and shoots.

Maybe you don't take the gun to work. Maybe instead you use the gun just to take out one person that really deserves it most. Maybe you learn to use a gun because you fear that person and know that he or she has several guns of his or her own, and it just makes sense to have one to protect yourself.

Guns don't kill people. People kill people, and people can choose to kill others using any sort of means they want, which includes guns. If guns didn't exist at all, people would still find ways to kill others. That's just a fact.

So, when I heard that my ex had bought a rifle and two handguns, it made me nervous. He had attempted suicide once, and the children and I had been really close to danger then. Who's to say he wouldn't shoot any of us if his proverbial cheese slid off his cracker again? He definitely wasn't the most stable-minded individual, and the children knew it and had experienced it as much as I had.

I had been thinking about getting a permit to conceal and carry for some time after I heard he had guns in his apartment. It still sounded off in my head, but so had the notion of ending him with a gun. It would be quick, he wouldn't see it coming, and that would be that.

I loved the idea of something quick. So simple, so easy, so impossible to escape alive when a bullet hits just the right spots in the body. A rifle could take off his head, and I could even make it look like a suicide if I managed it just right. Then again, it would be really hard to hide a rifle on my person when I'd see him during the day.

A handgun was more ideal. I'd need something with a large bore and caliber, though. I did research on a lot of different calibers and different kinds of bullets. It would seem that a Full Metal Jacket hollow point bullet was the roughest and ugliest of the bunch, leaving a ton of shrapnel and a very nasty wound that would be impossible to fix or clean up. Even though this type of bullet expanded on impact and splayed flesh like a butcher's knife, it meant that it would be the messiest sort of way of ending a life. The lethality of it was ideal, but the mess would leave a criminal forensics path so huge that it would make Moses parting the Red Sea look like a parlor trick.

Then someone would have to discover the body, and the evidence would be insurmountable. The blood splatter, for instance, would reveal height and girth of the shooter if shot from behind, and the height and trajectory of the bullet if shot from the front. Obviously, I would have to shoot from behind to avoid having him see what's coming and attempt to escape or call for help. I may have the ability to squish my fat rolls into a tight pair of jeans, but it wouldn't be enough to hide from the splatter evidence.

It would be seriously complicated trying to set up a shooting whereby he's shot from behind or at the temple while I'm standing in front. It would be great if I could make it look like a suicide with one of his own guns, but that would be truly impossible. Forensic science with guns and bullets has come such a long way that criminals using guns almost never escape the police and prosecution for very long.

Then there was the issue of having my own guns. They have to be registered, unless I buy "ghost guns", and that still makes me a suspect. There's always one other person in a gun transaction, no matter how you come by the gun, which means there is always someone that knows that you have the gun that was used in the shooting. If I got a permit to conceal and carry, that, too, makes it obvious, but you can't shoot a gun without a permit.

The biggest obstacle of all was that I had never shot a gun in my life. Not even a BB gun. I had heard about gun safety and hunter safety, but never shot a gun. I would have to get a permit, buy a gun, get a ton of ammo (which was seriously expensive), and shoot and shoot and shoot until my aim was perfect. There could be no room for errors when shooting a human target. Even then I would have to learn how to shoot a moving target in case he tried to run from me.

A silencer was necessary too. Only so many guns had silencers, and there were paper trails for purchasing those as well. I suppose a "ghetto silencer" made from a 2-liter soda bottle could work, but in all seriousness not everything you see on TV works. I could risk making a silencer from the soda bottle and then having it go very wrong at the last minute. That would require a lot of shooting practice and soda bottles, something I did not have time for or the stomach to swallow enough soda. You can silence a shot by shooting through a pillow as well, but if you are going to cover someone's head, face, neck or other part of the body with a pillow, you have to be in control of what that wriggling live person is doing before you can even shoot. Knocking him out would require a tertiary step in this more complicated plan to quietly shoot him.

What if I made it look like a drive-by shooting? It was completely laughable since a window rolled down would reveal my face. I was a really good actress from my early days in theater, and I knew how to use prosthetic makeup. I could don a huge fat suit to hide my own fat, a wig and a hat to hide my hair, and prosthetics to change the shape of my face, nose, eyes, chin, etc. That seemed like a lot of work and a lot of extra accessories and props to hide my identity in order to shoot my ex-husband at any hour of the day, not to mention that a car that wasn't mine would have to be part of the drive-by.

How would I dispose of the evidence gained by purchasing theatrical makeup and a fat suit, not to mention clothes to fit over the fat suit? Where would I get the car? You can't hide the car in a drive-by, and the plates would reveal who owned it. Masking the vehicle is not something I could manage, nor could I just get a getaway car with no plates, no history, and a non-descript appearance that I could change with a paint job.

If I hired someone to drive by where he worked or where I knew he would be at a given day and time, then I would also have a witness. You can't involve someone else in something like this or you spend your days looking over your shoulder wondering when that other person involved is going to tell the police. A shooting of this sort is too high-profile; it would get too much press and I would have to hide in plain sight or grab the kids and make a run for it. No, that was all way too complicated and far too messy an ordeal. Guns and shootings, as quick of a "solution" as they were, were far too cliché for what I was planning.

Wait—did I just say "planning"? Somehow thinking this thing out with guns involved had momentarily moved a fantasy of revenge and final resolution to an actual action. Was it the fact that guns were involved in the thought process and thus my emotional self was moved to actual planning stages instead of daydreaming? It was a scary thought since I had been so unsure up to a point that I'd ever really dig my heals in and do this. Yeah, I really wanted to, and yes, I really wanted him to just die and leave the kids and I alone, but I had been wavering so hard for so long. Now I was moved to *plan.*

I guess I'm actually doing this, but how is still the big question.

Chapter 7: Communicable Diseases

What an odd thought I had when I woke one morning. Killing someone with a communicable disease. You could do that. The science was sound, and you could just say that you didn't know how sick you were when you spread the illness. What diseases could I somehow pass to him without harming the kids or dying myself? What would work as a good route of transmission?

Clearly, I didn't want to sleep with him or swap spit with him or even share a drink with him. Transmission of virology or bacteria would require contact somehow. A lot of illnesses are transmitted through sneezing or blood. Even spitting in his face might work, but I'd have to be a carrier first. Putting myself at that much risk wasn't a good idea. Getting my hands on research samples of communicable diseases actually wasn't hard; I remember the samples in our bio lab in college and how easy it was to get such things through these specific locations or through professors who could order them.

I wasn't a professor, but I might be able to talk my way around one. I'd just have to convince a biology professor that I was doing some research or ask a lab researcher how to order samples for research. You'd be surprised how easy it is to order lab culture materials and viruses or bacteria online, shipped right to your doorstep.

Of course, I'd also have to have an antidote or vaccine for myself if I accidentally infected myself. I could probably still make the transmission process if I did contract whatevert I had purchased, but I'd still want to make myself better eventually. I imagined spending months working up my immunity and then waiting for the right moment to spring a disease on the Disease Himself. I have to say it made me chuckle just a little bit imagining it, and I have no doubt that most other people would be horrified that I could imagine such things, but they never lived through what I did. They wouldn't understand that survival of the worst things in life starts with imagining an end to that which caused you the worst pain and distress you've ever experienced.

I had heard of biologically matched health cures and medicines that fit into the DNA of an individual. These customized treatments were like magic to those suffering for years of their various afflictions. It was practically the stuff of espionage novels, but in reverse.

Then it occurred to me that you could create a genetically mutated and matched lethal strain of something to kill an individual. Use it to target certain cells in the body. The trouble lies in acquiring enough DNA to make and test these custom diseases, and my ex wasn't likely to just hand over skin, hair, or anything else to me. I wasn't likely to try and get DNA from him any other way either. Oh, that *would* be the perfect means of eliminating him because no one would ever suspect that he had died from a DNA-based customized disease that would only kill the one person it was meant to kill! Bonus points if I could have made it injectable into his Cola or sprinkled on a food I know he would eat. Yet, I would have to test it on the children's DNA too to make sure they would be completely safe to avoid accidental ingestion on their part. That would take months, even years to perfect, at which point the children would be full-grown, and I'd have to follow through on the plan because I had spent all that time developing it. Unless I could summon every last ounce of vengeance in my bones, I don't think this approach would ever work.

There were drawbacks to this method of killing too. Again, the children danced into my head. If they tried to come into my makeshift lab during the months of creating this imagined lethal pathogen, they could become ill and pass themselves. It was too horrible.

As far as a non-contact transmission, it would work just as easily as poison. Drop it in a drink and offer it to him. Sprinkle it into some food. Considering how listeria or E. coli, work, it wouldn't be hard to convince the police in their investigation that the deceased just ate a bad batch of cheese, meat, vegetables or fruit. Making sure only he ate the poison though was key.

I remembered a TV show where the bacteria that the murderer/murderess used in food made the children sick too. This villain made sure the children only got the smallest possible amount, nothing too lethal, just to convince a doctor in the emergency room that there's no way the villain would dare poison a child to eliminate a spouse. I couldn't imagine taking things that far, even if it would be more convincing in terms of an argument for accidental ingestion of E. coli, campylobacter, listeria, salmonella, and botulinum.

Out of all of these bacteria, probably the most likely to produce the best and most lethal results were salmonella or botulinum. As a nurse I could probably get my hands on some botulinum in the form of migraine injections and then either inject him or get it into food or drink. I could also raise chickens and have them tested for salmonella frequently to gather enough of the bacteria to make a lethal "treat" for my ex. Those two things were the easiest to do, but I also knew that they weren't always lethal.

However, I certainly could imagine him doubling over in a sweaty, agonizing, gut-blowing pain. Vomiting one minute and having an explosive anus the next was an image that provided me with some relief vicariously as I dwelled on whether or not it was possible to pass along a communicable disease via a virus or bacterial agent. Ultimately, I decided against it because there were too many factors that I could not control and getting enough of the bacteria or virus in his system to bump him off would take a lot of time and effort.

It always comes down to time and effort. When you want a revenge killing against someone who constantly tells you that you are the worst parent ever and you don't deserve your children, and who uses a third party to threaten your rights to your children, you can't find a lethal enough means that won't get you caught quite so quick. You can't find a "simple" solution to the problem to end the trauma, pain and suffering that won't take years to manufacture and plan and then finally execute. It was slowly, painfully becoming a moment of clarity for me that whatever and however I chose to take this bastard out, it would take time and effort to pick just the right means and just the right time to execute my plan. It was not going to be as simple as I had hoped, and the wild card factors involved were the kids.

Chapter 8: Transdermal and Transotic

Back when I was in college and just after we were married, I remember studying Shakespeare. I also remember being very pregnant at the time, feeling very uncomfortable in my own skin, and trying to do the assignments given by the theatre professors without drawing attention to my growing belly. I was so tired all the time, and so angry too. My "darling" husband was busy spending every dime we made on himself, and the bills were growing faster than the infant in my abdomen. Every month we were in the red before we even paid rent. Every day I would go to class all day and go to work third shift all night and figure out when I could sleep.

Truth be told, I was taking short naps at work. That was not a good thing to do because I was expected to be awake all night, but I was so tired, and I knew I needed to be awake for classes the next day. I was depressed too, because the person I married should have been looking out for me and the unborn child and should have been more supportive. Instead, he was busy buying fishing equipment, a boat, professional photography equipment, computer games, virtual computer currency and in-game purchases, and dozens of other "hobbies" he'd pick up for a month and put down for all of time. His manic behavior and his spending were damaging to our relationship, and I'd get so frustrated with him that we'd fight for a bit, but then the exhaustion of pregnancy and my schedule would cause me to quit the fight sooner than later.

I can remember studying some of Shakespeare's most well-known plays in class then and telling a classmate how my dingbat of a husband would tell me that I "only had to do this for nine months, and it would be easier after the baby arrived." My professor overheard me and said, "Oh, is that what he thinks?" and we both laughed. My then-husband was stupid enough to think that after the mother has ejected the child from her womb, it's easy from there. Moron.

I took consolation in that few weeks by reading up on Hamlet and "the play that shall not be named (that Scottish play)". Hamlet supplied me with the vicarious release of anger through the means of death used by Hamlet's uncle to kill Hamlet's father and assume the throne. The sleeping king had a few drops of a poison set into his ear, which circled into his brain and the poor sleeping king died almost immediately.

A transotic death of an unsuspecting victim gave me the idea. What kind of tinctures could possibly kill someone when dripped into the human ear? It turns out that these were not poisons, but toxins, and that they passed through the ear drum and into the inner ear, following the auditory nerve to the brain and resulted in a very painful death. My theatre professors were quite thorough in their dissecting and teaching of this method, and I relished it.

A nerve toxin delivered to the ear would have only worked while we were still married. I missed a golden opportunity on that one, to be sure, since after the divorce we kept our distance as much as possible. Well, actually I kept my distance because I didn't enjoy volatile, toxic, abusive, and demented people in my life.

Then I realized that transotic means of death was remarkably similar to *transdermal.* Since the turn of this century, modern medicine had begun to look for ways to turn all sorts of medications into transdermal patches. Too many of the wrong kind of patch could kill or overstimulate or even reduce one's ability to avoid doing stupid and dangerous things. There were patches for diabetes, patches to control one's nicotine habit, and patches to stop a heart attack in mid attack (nitroglycerin patches) that you could apply to the body. The medicine in the patches soaked through the skin to the bloodstream below and went to work.

Oddly enough, this modern idea wasn't all that new. Fairy tales like Snow White involved poisoned bodice strings and poisoned hair combs where the poison or toxin sunk into the wearer's skin and killed them. It just took a twenty-first century pharmaceutical company to reproduce the simplest wearable item as both a means of life-saving medication or life-stealing poison. Switching out a few patches of nicotine control with nitroglycerin would be easy if he asked me to pick up some of his patches for him, but lately he hadn't asked me to do that. I found out that he had given up smoking and switched to vaping.

When I heard he had switched to vaping, I immediately got my wheels spinning. If you remember that scene in the Grinch Christmas movie where his face smirks as he gets an awful idea, that's exactly how I pictured my inner self at that moment. Vaping was still essentially transdermal, except that the oil for vaping was transferred into a vape pen.

The vape oil itself could be laced with something nasty. It would have to be a high content of nasty so that when transformed into a vapor and inhaled it would not decrease in efficacy. In fact, many of my prior ideas with poisons, toxins, biological agents, etc., all came flooding back to me. All it would take is dosing a vape oil refill of his favorite flavor or nicotine level and then leaving it in his car or introducing it as something he dropped by accident. It was fiendish, and I was quite enjoying the daydream about it.

I really thought this was it; the transdermal approach via a vape oil. Simple, uncomplicated, and brilliant. I almost fell in love with the plan entirely until I slept soundly for the first time in years and woke up to some stark realizations and flaws in the plan.

I'm not a chemist. It's like the daydream I had about being a sniper and shooting him from a church rooftop four miles away and having no one suspect I did it. I wasn't a sniper either. Not a chemist; can't get the dosage exactly right for the vape cartridge. There was also the tiny issue of trying to figure out exactly what kind of vape oil he vaped, where he typically bought it, what it looked like, and making sure my fingerprints on the cartridge and a paper trail didn't lead the police back to me. It's not like I could don gloves and hand off the cartridge to my ex; that would look very weird to him indeed.

I suppose I could say that I didn't want to accidentally get nicotine juice on my hands, but I doubt he'd fall for it. If I placed it in his car where he'd "accidentally" find it, I had to avoid being seen, and I would have to make sure the cartridge couldn't freeze or melt in a cold or hot car. I don't think it would be a problem with the kids, but what did I know about leaky vape cartridges? Did they leak, and how often?

Too many questions to resolve meant that my glory was short-lived. It would have been so perfect if it weren't so tricky. Then another transdermal idea floated into my brain.

Clothing. All those stories and murder mysteries and TV shows had characters dying of clothing that was laced with toxins. Only the toxins were damaging to the wearer; not to someone who wasn't wearing the clothing. The clothing could burn flesh, cause disfigurement, or even a rapid and unpleasant death. Ricin could do that. So could cinnabar, from which mercury is extracted and which was the lethal liquid used to paint the insides of clothing used in ancient human sacrifice. It was such a long, slow, painful death from these clothing items, and it would only take seconds for him to realize that my gift of a toxic shirt was doing something nasty to him. He would have that off and reach for a phone before it would take full effect.

So many good ideas, so many lovely deaths in history, books, stories, and works of Shakespeare. It's just sad that things only worked out to a certain extent in those stories, books, plays, and historical events, and that it just would not work out now.

"Keep thinking!" I told myself. *"The perfect ending to such an awful being has to exist."*

Chapter 9: Suffocation Several Ways

You're probably already thinking that the ship has sailed on suffocation, right? Most people end a life using a pillow to suffocate, and it is extremely difficult to do because the person will fight you all the way. Even a sleeping person will wake up and realize he or she can't breathe and begin to fight back, kicking and slapping and grabbing blindly at that which halts his or her ability to breathe. Plastic bags around the head have killed toddlers and small children by accident for decades, and the bags still carry warning signs that they can kill and should not be placed over one's head. With adults, a plastic bag over one's head only suffocates if the victim can't effectively remove it in time. It means that my ex would have to be fully restrained in order to be suffocated with a pillow or suffocated with a plastic bag, and I would have to be close enough to him for an extended period of time to make that work.

So, you wouldn't be wrong to say that suffocation was not an option anymore. What you may not have counted on was that I'm really thorough in my research. I found that there were multiple nerve agents that can cause suffocation all on their own. A couple are untraceable, too, which got my wheels spinning again.

If I wanted to go "old school," a nerve toxin from the second world war could do it. Sarin, or GB, is 26 times more lethal than a dose of cyanide, and cyanide is pretty lethal in and of itself. Sarin would take a tiny amount and cause him to slip into an arrested muscle state, stopping the diaphragm, the heart, and the lungs all at once. All of the muscles in the body would immediately arrest and never move again. He would move from salivation to lacrimation (crying) to urination to defecation (peeing and pooping himself—nice!) to emesis (vomiting) before final death thralls. While he gasps for air, he would be very aware of his surroundings but unable to speak, move, or reach for a phone to call for help. The obstacle to delivering the sarin, however, was getting it into him.

He could breathe it, eat it, inject it, or drink it. I had already previously ruled out eating and drinking to avoid accidental death to the children, at least while they still had to spend time with him. Injecting it would require metering a dose and suspending it in a liquid that could then be injected somehow into him. The idea of the spy cane injection came back. Breathing it also left the kids exposed, so injecting it would really be the only option.

Other nerve agents that lead to suffocation and arrested breathing include a British manufactured toxin known simply as VX. VX is even more potent than sarin if all the documentation is to be believed. A couple drops is all it takes, and within *seconds* rather than minutes the target is eliminated. It's the type of deadly manmade warfare agent that, if the agent were a person, it would be the angriest woman on the planet with a death stare a thousand miles long.

I found that certain prescription sedative drugs are also classified as neurotoxins. I was aware of some medications that have equal power to cure or kill, but it didn't dawn on me that some of the prescription drugs my ex-husband took for sleep or anti-anxiety could be lethal. They could even be made to look like an intentional overdose. This included the clonazepam and fluoxetine he took for his mood disorders and would frequently stop taking "when he felt much better."

It reminded me of when we first started dating. He had made dinner for me at his place. He was not a good cook, and the chopped boiled egg sauce the recipe instructed him to pour over boiled asparagus as a side dish was unpleasant. I tried my best not to grimace, and then excused myself at one point when I felt nauseous and thought I might throw up. While in his bathroom, I tried to find a towel to dry my hands and pat down my face, but instead found several pill bottles in the drawers in his bathroom vanity. Each one was labeled with a medication I knew well, because many patients in my care were taking similar mood drugs.

These bottles were quite full, but the dates on them were older than a month. That should have been my first warning sign to leave and not date this one any further. However, if I was being honest here, I had to take a mood stabilizer once or twice in my life too, just to get over a hump, so I dismissed it. It did come up in conversation later when I asked him why he had full bottles of these pills in his bathroom and that the bottles seemed rather old.

He replied, "Because I'm happy now that you are here in my life, and I don't need any other happy pills except you."

I guess that line worked on some people, but it actually made me queasy. I think that queasiness showed on my face more than I wanted it to because he asked me if he had said something wrong. I informed him that a person's presence in his life should never replace a medication that he needed to improve his emotional well-being and I didn't like being his "new source of medicinal joy." He laughed it off, didn't take me seriously, and said he'd start taking his pills again soon.

Turns out, he stopped taking the pills for a long time. When he wasn't medicated, he was a nightmare. I often thought he might be bipolar just because of the many swings of his moods and how violent and hostile he would get when he would self-medicate some other way. Not surprisingly, when we divorced, he cited that he no longer found me to be the source of his joy and that pills might be better after all. How ironic.

In fact, he constantly looked for mood lifters outside of himself. He was never wrong, and there was never anything wrong with *him*. If someone else stopped making him happy, he simply would ignore that person and look for someone else to make him happy. He would only go to counseling if the counselor validated that others in his life were wrong and that he was right. It's why he continually abandoned his wife and child (and later children); he expected others to make him happy in ways no other human being could ever really make someone happy.

Even his affair in Alabama only made him happy for about two weeks because the sex was constant. After that, he felt controlled, isolated, dirty, and used. He later told me that he began to feel cheap, and he didn't like being told that he couldn't even go outside of the apartment they shared to get a meal. I almost felt sorry for him until he revealed that the only thing he didn't really mind was the near constant unprotected sex. He repeatedly put himself in danger with someone he didn't really know that well for seven weeks and then decided to just come home to his wife and children like nothing happened. Foolishly, I let him.

When he came home, he went back on his pills that had been prescribed for him before he ran off to be with her. His mood stabilized somewhat, but his participation in childcare and parenting responsibilities and looking after the house while I worked double shifts again was dismal at best. The house was always trashed when I came home, the babies were always in dirty diapers and not much else while they crawled and ran around the house unsupervised, and he sat in the corner of the living room on his computer again.

I digress. What he needed was a larger pill load than he was taking. He still needed that but wasn't likely to take it. Maybe a death by fluoxetine (more commonly known as Prozac) or his chosen benzodiazepines would be suitable if I could get enough of these pills into him.

When our daughter reached her early teens, something else happened that made me think that the death by tranquilizer was a fitting end. She was initially incredibly difficult to manage, but she had faced a lot of trauma early in her life and again at the hands of five adult men posing as those who should be trustworthy with her care, namely police officers and teachers. Instead, she was sorely abused and availed of her civil rights by those who had no training in how to help her and refused to listen to me, the person who had raised her most of her life.

What happened that spring and summer was something that made me choke back tears and be very fearful for her. Any time her father interceded, he would force her to take his own prescription benzodiazepines. She would sink into a thousand-mile hazed stare, unaware of her surroundings, and then fall into a deep slumber for several hours. When it was his weekend to spend time with her during this eventful period in her life, he would frequently make her take his pills and knock her out. The sad part is that he would admit to me that he had done this, and he had no remorse about it at all.

That's when I began to consider force-feeding him tons of his own pills to see how he enjoyed being drugged out of his mind. He would probably like it until he started to slip from consciousness never to return. How much fluoxetine or clonazepam was lethal? I would need to pump over 14,000mg of clonazepam into his system to make it lethal. That was tricky, considering that most prescription doses never exceeded 20mg, and I was certain his dosage prescribed for him was much smaller. I would need five *years'* worth of this drug to make him OD. Sure, I was a nurse, but there's no way I could "acquire" that much of a Schedule IV drug to use in this fashion without someone noticing that it was missing from the medication room at work.

As for fluoxetine, more commonly known by its brand name of Prozac, that was a different story. Somewhere between 520mg and 8 grams is lethal, depending on the person's tolerance levels. If they take it a long time, the amount has to be stepped up regularly to continue to get the same "happy" state while under a psychiatrist's watchful eye. My ex took it on and off, sometimes at the highest prescribed dose allowed. I just didn't know if I could adequately calculate the right amount to be lethal for him. If it wasn't lethal, a hospital could easily pump his stomach and save him. Then that one shot at ending him would be it where this drug was concerned.

Supposing he still had a bottle of 80mg of fluoxetine laying around. Even so, he would need to consume somewhere between an entire month's worth of pills and two- or three-months' worth of pills to be remotely fatal. There was also the fact that he would go peacefully, happily, with a stupid euphoric grin on his face and not an ounce of pain or remorse for everything he did to us while he was alive. No, that definitely was not the kind of death blow I wanted to give him. That was the kind of "kind" death blow Dr. Kevorkian delivered when patients were tired of living in pain and wanted to go peacefully. Where my ex was concerned, I decided that this level of neurotoxin in the form of medication was a non-starter.

Other neurotoxins that existed and were well within reach were lighter fluid (benzene) and anti-freeze (ethylene glycol). If he had been smoking still instead of vaping, I could look at the lighter fluid as a means of elimination, except that it had to be injected to be effective. Several lighters would need to be emptied and several syringes filled to make it work. That was a lot of needle marks that could not be explained away during an autopsy. As it turns out, he eventually did resume smoking, but the benzene approach would require a lengthy kidnapping, sedation, and repeated injections with healing to look like the "track marks" drug addicts had in their arms.

Anti-freeze was an idea I had been considering before. It reared its head again when something bizarre happened to our son's cat. The animal wasn't even seven years old, but my ex had fed it to excess hoping it would die faster. He didn't like the animal, and the animal clearly didn't like him as evidenced by the frequent and vicious claw attacks to my ex's legs and feet. The animal knew what a nasty piece of work my ex was, and he reacted as any excellent judge of character would.

Still, my ex kept the cat around because of our son. Our son loved his cat; they were best buddies. That cat would snuggle up to our son and sit quietly next to him as the boy read to him. It was so sweet to see this cat take to the boy, and the boy to the cat.

But my ex had it in for the cat from the get-go. He spent four years trying to fatten the animal to death. When that failed, he put the cat on a diet and limited its food intake to make it lose weight as fast as possible. The cat continued to show his disdain for my ex with lots of deep claw cuts.

One weekend, when the children were home with me, the cat met his end. The poor animal suddenly was very sick and could not urinate to save its life. It cried piteously and would not be comforted because his favorite boy wasn't there. My ex took it into the emergency animal hospital (more likely to avoid a cruelty to animals charge or to make it look good for our son). It was determined that this very young adult cat had crystals in its urine, a condition most cats do not develop this early in life.

The bills for the next week to save the cat and give my son a chance to say goodbye fell to me, of course. It took weeks to get my ex to pay half of the bill from the animal hospital. We tried everything, but it was clear that the cat had accepted its fate and was going to leave this earth. The cat was just waiting for his boy to be okay with the cat's death.

When my son realized that his cat was in pain and could not really be saved, he let go. He shared one last heartbreaking moment of reading to his cat in the vet's office, and then they put the animal to sleep. He was buried in a beautiful animal coffin made by a family member and placed in the family pet cemetery in the country.

Shortly thereafter, I realized that urine crystals are also the direct result of ethylene glycol poisoning. In a bowl of water, a few drops were enough to kill any animal. We had frequently used it to kill rodents on the farm, and an occasional barn cat would die as the result of eating the poisoned rodent. Having been the only one left at home with the cat that weekend, it seemed like my ex took full advantage of ending the cat's life. My vet confirmed that the crystals in the cat's kidneys and bladder could definitely be caused by poisoning with anti-freeze.

My ex had just upped his "game" by killing the one thing his son loved more than him; a cat that loved the boy and hated my ex. The cat that had caused a division between father and son was gone. The sad part was that the animal was now in the ground, and there was no one within 150 miles of us that could have performed a necropsy to prove it even if we had wanted to exhume the cat's body. This was the final sign that my ex could be very dangerous indeed, and that he would stop at nothing to force a stronger bond between himself and our son. I wasn't sure who was at greatest risk of harm; me and my daughter, or my son. Either way, we all needed to be on guard and careful, even if I couldn't say a single word to my children about what I suspected had happened to the cat.

The thought of turning the tables and poisoning my ex with anti-freeze seemed to be poetic justice. A little taste of his own deadly medicine is exactly what he needed. The delivery method had to be exactly right so that the kids would never fall victim in the process. Since the anti-freeze was already quite sweet, I just had to find the right food item to hide the taste of the anti-freeze. I decided to shelve this neurotoxin as a major possibility for future use. Suffocation by neurotoxin actually seemed feasible.

Chapter 10: Death by Fire

Dying in a fire is a horrible way to die, but not if you're someone who clearly deserved it. I must admit that I'm a bit of a pyromaniac; I love setting things ablaze and watching fire dance. Fire takes on its own life, dancing around and consuming everything it touches. Maybe it's why death by fire at the stake was so popular an execution during the hundreds of witch trials in Europe and the Americas. It was both punitive for those being burned and entertainment for those that enjoyed a good roaring fire.

Question was, could I kill by fire? It's not to say that I couldn't, but you had to be a truly sadistic personality to light someone ablaze and watch it happen. The smell of burning flesh might be too much for me too. Burning my hair once by accident when I came too close to a stove burner was a smell I'll never forget. I didn't like that smell. I've burned fingers on grills, burners, and even clothing irons, and the smell was not pleasant even though those burns are quite mild.

So, torching my ex completely could only be done a couple of ways. One, I knock him out and do the whole "Burning Man" thing with him inside a pile of wood and claim I didn't know he was there. Two, I could knock him out and set him on fire somewhere else, but it could put a lot of other people in danger if the flames spread to woods or houses and such. I could commit an act of arson and set his apartment on fire, but it would require *weeks* of careful observation to see when the neighbors living downstairs from him left their apartment and were not home. I also didn't think it fair to burn down somebody else's property and abode just to erase my ex from existence.

Funny, isn't it? I'm more considerate of total strangers, not knowing if they are equally as twisted and nasty as my ex. What if his neighbors were just as bad? He had drug dealers living downstairs for a time. It would have been okay to burn them out. After all, they were supplying crack and heroin to the local addicts who would inject themselves in the park down the street and then leave their used needles in the grass around the playground. Ugly mess, that. Even the local police were disgusted with how the local addicts were leaving dangerous items around for kids and pets to encounter. They did a whole news story on it, too.

Unfortunately, the drug dealers moved on. They took their boat, their Cadillac Escalade with the darkened windows, their convertible and their motorcycle out of the driveway and left one day. The new neighbors seemed much quieter and kept to themselves; you know, like typical small town serial killers. I hadn't seen them once in the whole time I was dropping off and picking up the kids after their father broke his leg. Usually when it comes to people who keep to themselves like that, you're not likely to bang on the door and say hello. Even though I would have loved to notify them that their upstairs neighbor was a real piece of work, I leave those sleeping dogs lie.

If I could establish when the neighbors were not present at home, but my ex was, a little arson would require some very careful planning. You certainly can't walk down the street with a gas can in one hand and a lighter or matches in the other! You can't park your car within four blocks of the place you intend to torch either. There was a set of railroad tracks that ran behind the house that served as the two apartments. One might try to sneak up on the tracks and attempt arson at night.

However, you would have to place the gas or other ignitable fluid in deep cover and make sure it couldn't tip over before you came back in the evening. I'd have to cover myself in tight black clothing too. The car would have to be parked several blocks away, like at the local pharmacy where it would be obviously seen in case police wanted to check cameras to check up on something like that. I would have to wear some brightly colored clothes over the top of the black clothes, take a large purse with me to put the colorful clothes and gas can into after the fact, and then sneak around behind buildings and out of sight of security cameras and street cameras to get to the tracks. I'd walk along the tracks until I got close to the ex's apartment and then ducking into trees to remove the colorful clothing before emerging all in black.

I could just hear the old Hitchcock eerie music playing in my head as I went about my "shadow ops" mission. Those old movie soundtracks with their sinister and foreboding tones were ideal for this kind of death. Horror and suspense movie makers could picture this, and so could I.

I also thought about how I could just use the colorful clothing for igniting the fire, but then realized that I would be seen all in black on the way back to my car. I could leave the gas can abandoned near the tracks, but only if it had been left clean of fingerprints and trace evidence (e.g., clothing threads, glove powder, etc.). The gas can would have to look really old and beaten down, as though it had been discarded a long time ago and just happened to be in the weeds along the railroad tracks. So much evidence to hide while being out in the open to burn down an apartment house in the middle of the night seemed to take a lot of consideration.

There was the fact that I would have to duck and cover from the police during their patrols, unless I could figure out how and when they patrolled. Great, more research. The kids couldn't be left alone, even if they were sound asleep in their beds. It would be just my luck that as I went to set fire to the ex's apartment, someone would break into my home and put the kids in danger. Death by fire was proving more difficult by the second.

For that short time that the ex vaped, there was no way to make fire look like an accident. After some time, he gave up vaping and returned to cigarettes. I remembered when we were married, and he had fallen asleep in the recliner more than once with a cigarette in his hand or on his lips. He had burned holes in his clothes and put a couple of burns on the arms of the recliner. I was really angry about that because the recliner had belonged to my grandfather who had passed away shortly after my son was born. Here the careless boob almost incinerated the chair and nearly started a fire in the apartment. It would be so easy to make it look like he had fallen asleep again with a cigarette in his hand if I could manage to knock him out and put him on his couch or in a comfy chair. How reliable would it be to start an accidental fire with just a cigarette? If I could pull that off, I'd still have to keep my own DNA off the cigarette and make it look like he was the one who had actually been smoking it.

A long cigarette holder that ladies in Old Hollywood used to use for smoking would help me start the cigarette's burn. Removing it and swirling it around in his unconscious lips would put his DNA on it. He had to stay asleep the whole time, and then he would have to remain asleep even as the fires burned higher around him. The problem would be in getting into his apartment on some premise of talking and trying to get him to shirk the mutual restraining order against each other imposed by divorce court documents seemed almost insurmountable. Yet the burning cigarette and accidental death by fire would appear quite plausible, and the slow fire would at least give neighbors time to get out of the building.

Wait, I think I just debunked my own thought process. If the fire were slow enough, it wouldn't matter if he slept through it all. People would notice a burning smell and call for help. A small fire burning through the floor to the neighbors' ceiling below would give the fire department enough time to put the fire out. At best, he might die from smoke inhalation. At worst, he'd survive with melted scar tissue for skin and the ability to point the finger at me.

Damn! I used to think criminals were so dumb because they never thought out each step of their plan. The truth is, someone could be a very smart criminal and still realize the dozen different ways their plans could really go sideways in a hurry. How could anyone execute a revenge death on an ex-spouse if every which way you turned there was another unexpected plot twist and more complications?

I wondered if he still used lit cigarettes to burn himself. If it wasn't cigarettes, he'd just cut himself with a razor blade. Considering all of the insanity I had lived through with him, he certainly left the door wide open for possible death scenes that would look so "innocent", believable, and probable that very few would even question what really happened. Trying to pick just one way to die was almost as difficult as trying to avoid being accused of the jerk's death. A lot of situations that hearkened back to when we were married made circles around me as I thought things through, and the time continued to slip away from me.

The truth is, he had said he wanted to be cremated. I think it was in his will. I would just be hurrying it along a bit, although I didn't like a certain aspect of my death by fire plot. I knew he wanted to go out on a funeral pyre, with the mistaken notion that he would be burned like a Viking. Vikings actually never died that way, so he would be dying the way he wanted to and I, his ex-wife, would be granting his final wish. This "yuck factor" is precisely why I decided that death by fire was not what he would get.

Chapter 11: Invisible Death

This is a very intriguing way to cause a death. Anything and everything that would result in death that you cannot see, nor can you figure out what caused it falls under this category. I loved the idea of an invisible death because it was so sci-fi, so creepy, so perfect for someone that walked around looking like he was normal when behind closed doors and away from visible eyes of the public he was such a monster.

Gaseous invisible death included radon and carbon monoxide. Both could be found in a home in elevated amounts. The older the structure, the more likely there were these gases present. I didn't remember if he had monoxide detectors in his apartment; most people don't. They don't usually install radon detectors either. People go for the main detector, the ones that detect smoke and fire. They are never thinking about invisible gases that could make them sick or kill them.

Radon would be too difficult because it would have to be collected in a large enough amount and pumped only into his apartment. Carbon monoxide was less difficult to acquire and probably easier to release through some opening in his windows or under the door. Being seen would be a problem, so it really wasn't that invisible. However, the cause of death would be deemed accidental by way of carbon monoxide poisoning. If I could avoid being seen and manage to not trigger the kids' suspicion of me, this was another viable option.

There were other types of invisible deaths too. An old tale of a CIA agent killing with an ice bullet was especially intriguing. Ice has long since been the bane of man, since it causes you to fall, injure yourself, even cut yourself if you crack the ice into jagged sheets. A sharp enough ice dagger could slice a major blood vessel. If you could recreate an ice bullet with enough integrity to pass through flesh without melting, that could work too.

The reason why ice is such a good death weapon is because the weapon melts. Police would see water melted or encounter water in the wound, but no one would suspect an ice weapon would fit the profile or be named the cause of death. They would be searching in earnest for years for a knife that had the right blade edge and style, or for the bullet and gun that never seemed to materialize.

A large icicle hanging from the house or from the eaves around his apartment could work if the icicle were very hard, very pointed, and very heavy. The blow with this weapon would have to go through the eye socket into the brain or find its way through the sweet spot in the back of the skull where the first neck vertebra meets the bottom of the back of the skull. This latter option has an open space just right for a cutting, slicing, or dagger-like weapon to completely sever the entire spinal cord from the rest of the body.

If the brain can't communicate with the heart, lungs, and diaphragm, the person dies and can only be rescued if placed on a ventilator the rest of his natural life. Again, this required close contact, but it was becoming more and more obvious to me that any method of death I chose would require a short distance in close quarters to actually be effective. I didn't want to consider that or even think about it, but I knew that if I were going to carry this out, it would have to place me in close proximity to someone I wanted to be a million miles away from.

Getting a bullet to pass through bone was impossible. It's been tried and debunked. But as a nurse, I knew the softest areas of the human body where penetration could cause the most damage. I'd have to hit the femoral artery, the carotid, the brachial artery, or pass the ice bullet into the brain via the underside of the jaw and at a 45-degree angle. The precision of this ice bullet would require very close contact, same as a regular metal bullet. Being that I couldn't hit the broad side of a barn with most guns, I might botch it with an ice bullet.

There was also the small matter of making an ice bullet propel out of a firearm at a speed sufficient to push the ice bullet through flesh. No ice bullet could survive the force of a standard gun. I would have to construct some sort of "ghost gun" from materials that could force the icy projectile forward without melting it or causing it to shatter. One possibility was to use some sort of cannister device with pressure built up from behind and a trigger release, like a pressure washer or helium tank. The construction of such would take some time to perfect, and I would have to be able to convert it back to its original intended use after the frozen bullet met its target. Quickly assembled, and more quickly disassembled and reassembled into something else would be necessary. Years and years were required to research it and turn it into the perfect weapon.

The integrity of an ice bullet was still difficult to predict. A popular forensic science and mystery show posited that frozen *blood* would hold together better than just water and deliver twice the blow. Resisting the quick deterioration when exposed to the warmer air, the frozen blood bullet would hold together right up to cutting into human flesh. Additionally, any frozen blood product that didn't match the blood type of the victim would cause the victim's own body to turn on itself like a rejected organ. Having access to chilled blood at the hospital, it wouldn't take much to get a little and deep freeze it in the perfect mold to make a bullet for the weapon I would have to craft for it.

It would take doctors several hours to figure out why the patient wasn't responding to treatments for the wound if he were found and rescued before bleeding out. It could be slow and agonizing, a vision of death most apropos for the likes of my ex.

Another invisible death option wasn't ice, but *wood*. Initially, when airports began banning firearms on planes, would-be terrorists crafted weapons from plastic and wood. The plastic components were well disguised in a carry-on, while the wood weapons could not be detected going through airport security. A wooden bullet had the gun powder packed into the back end in order to propel it forward from the wooden gun.

Once the bullet hit the target, one only had to retrieve the bullet and burn it. When the gun was also wooden, the gun could be burned as well. The ashes could be scattered on the water, in the wind, or anywhere else they could not be recovered in several days' time. No weapon, no trace. No trace, no evidence. No evidence, no proof. Police and investigators would be lost looking for the missing bullet and the gun that fired it. The wooden bullet would just need a very sharp tip and enter a part of the body where it would be easy to retrieve or pass through the body and retrieved another way.

I'm reminded of another type of invisible death. A story about a sleeping husband being killed with a frozen leg of lamb by a vengeful wife who then serves up the leg of lamb to the investigating police officers is a delightful tale of vengeance, to be sure. If you *eat* the weapon or evidence, how can you be caught?

The biggest issue with killing with a frozen edible weapon was that someone would surely recognize the parallels between that story and this murder. Not all police officers go through life avoiding reading classic pieces of modern literature, which would make this invisible death a tricky one. I would have to gamble on an entire police force looking for a blunt force weapon that had already been consumed and bones disposed of if bones were involved in the weapon. You could definitely kill someone with canned food too, but that left trace evidence on the cans. It had to be something heavy, frozen, and completely edible. Considering that I wasn't about to make a complete special dinner for my ex-husband, this option was nixed for the inability to execute it without suspicion or recognition of its origins.

I also heard of a most unusual invisible death where a man died as a result of a powerful kick to the groin with steel-toed boots. There's some confusion as to whether or not this is possible, but because it has been used as a reasonable cause of death on a coroner's report, it actually is possible.

Essentially what happens is that I would have to wrap my toes in the perfect cushion of protection and then wear the heaviest steel-toed boots I can find. I would have to practice kicking with precision such I would not lose my balance in delivering the fatal kick. The heaviness of the boots tends to throw off one's center of gravity and one's balance, making it quite difficult to kick and kick hard enough with the boots on. Leg strength involving powerful muscles and abdominal strength to keep me balanced when my leg swings out were steps I would have to take to be in the best possible shape for this kind of bizarre death.

The idea is to nail a man in the testicles with exceptional force in a single blow. In so doing, the scrotum is ruptured, the testicles send a reverberation of waves into the abdomen where the intestines rupture, and if kicked hard enough, the waves of force travel to the heart and make the heart explode as well. It has to be done in one perfect, powerful kick with no misses and no second guessing. It's unlikely that a male victim would just stand there and take a kick to the family jewels without flinching or attempting to protect himself, but it's the type of freaky death I found interesting and quite fitting.

My mind flashed back to a moment on our honeymoon. I went to tour some historical sites for the day. I had hoped he would come with, since we were meeting some very special people enroute and we would probably never meet again. He declined, stating he wanted to just relax at the hotel. I later found out upon returning from my adventures that he wasn't "in the mood" for anything most newlyweds are up for. He had also left the hotel to visit the city's notorious red-light district, and while I didn't think anything of it at the time, I found out later what had taken place.

Not even married a month, and he had taken full advantage of my absence in a distant location from home to engage a prostitute. The bizarre thing is that he told me about seeing prostitutes in broad daylight where he went, and that he could recognize them for what they were right away. This had disturbed me at the time, but I chalked it up to the fact that he was just trying to get a rise out of me. As it turns out, he had engaged at least one of the prostitutes he described in a back-alley act in accordance with the area of that city that had made its prostitutes quite famous and infamous. I didn't discover the truth until years later, and by then I had already been betrayed several times over. Discovering his earlier escapades only made me cringe instead of feeling the red-hot anger I might have felt at the time.

Therefore, an invisible death by a massive trauma blow to his testicles would have probably been one of the most ideal deaths ever. I wished it were easier to deliver that blow, but he would see it coming and block my foot. He would know I was trying to kick him where it would hurt most, and he wouldn't give me a second chance at it ever again. It would have been so fitting, considering that this invisible death only leaves internal damage and marks on the scrotum with no other visible signs of murder whatsoever. A blow to his nuts with such force was so apropos that I just kept it in the back of my mind for amusement. It helped me smile every time I faced something awful with him later on.

Chapter 12: Death by Explosion

Everyone has had at least one person in their lives that they imagined exploding into a fiery final stage. In most cases it is probably your boss, who annoys you to no end and who you would gladly like to see spontaneously combust and leave you with a sense of satisfaction and peace. For others, it might be that one in-law you can't stand. For me, and probably for dozens or hundreds of others like me, it's the ex.

Any time I was especially angry with my husband, and I could not sleep for all the burning anger I felt. I had to imagine him exploding into thousands of little bits. Better still was when I imagined him turning into an instant pile of ash in an explosion. It helped soothe my raw nerves and calm me enough to sleep. The next day I would try to forget why I was mad, but he would usually do something else to push my buttons because he enjoyed being in a fight regardless of what the fight was about.

I didn't enjoy fighting. I didn't enjoy being so angry that I felt like a medieval executioner choosing which methods and weapons to use to end his life. I spent countless hours being this angry, while he spent countless hours amused at how furious I was. It was a vicious circle, a merry-go-round with saw blades spinning instead of animals on which to ride. I didn't want to be on that. I wanted to get off and not get back on ever again. I wanted to heal, but every time I tried, he would turn around and do something else to jumpstart all of the pain, anger, feelings of hurt and betrayal, lack of trust, and memories of lies all over again. I knew the only true way to start over, start clean, and feel refreshed and healed was to remove him from the face of the earth.

So, while I imagined him blowing up quite often, I never thought I would consider actual means of death by explosion to be a viable option. There are so many ways to carry this out too. Pipe bombs, dirty bombs, timed bombs, dynamite, and plastic explosives, just to name a few. Luring someone into a building right before it is blown up or imploded works too.

Going about it requires a lot of thought. You can get detailed plans for all kinds of bombs now that the internet is a free-for-all place to get information. Pipe bombs can be strapped to car bumpers or inserted into an exhaust pipe. Car bombs are wired into the ignition. Molotov cocktails hurled through a window take out the space in which they are thrown, but you have to throw them just right. Grenades sold as army surplus are ridiculously easy to come by. War profiteers sell explosive devices and parts as "souvenirs" of different wars and never deactivate the items they sell. Grenade launchers and rocket launchers are sold at weapons expos and online all the time.

The more sophisticated version of death by explosion involves going on the dark web and hiring a hacker to reroute a government missile and point it at your ex's house. As much fun as that might be, it could take out more than just his abode and him. It could take out an entire city block. For me, that wouldn't' be so bad considering that his sister lived right next door to him, and I didn't like her or any of his family any better than he. What bothered me was that there was a nice, retired couple on the other side, and the dark web plot would hurt them.

Luring him into a building that was set to be demolished may not work. I would have to arrange a meeting with him and ask him to meet me in this building for some bizarre but believable reason. I would have to know the exact time the building would be demolished, but also when the demolition expert would not be in the building. Most demo crews would do a walk-through of the building to make sure no one would be trapped in the rubble and sometimes the entire block around that building would be closed off with a security fence to prevent injury to bystanders. He would be too suspicious of that anyway, so I passed.

I could acquire C-4 easily enough, but detonators were not commonly sold or as easily acquired. By keeping the detonators out of public sale, the government is able to prevent everyday people from blowing up a lot of things. It makes sense, but it also made this option impossible without making friends with a licensed demolition expert or military explosives expert.

Pipe bombs and dirty bombs were probably the easiest. All you needed was some plumbing pipe that was sold through local hardware stores and/or a ton of nails and screws or bits of glass sharp enough to slice flesh on impact. Of course, people did survive dirty bombs, so maybe an effectively placed pipe bomb was the better option. Attaching it to his car so that the car would flip, explode, burst into flames and toast what was left of him inside made for quite an imaginative scene. It was the stuff Hollywood stunt persons dream of, plus the slow and easy acquisition of these items from multiple stores over the course of a year would mean that it was less susceptible to discovery, especially if I paid in cash for the items.

Remote control detonators hadn't figured into my plans, but they were worth considering. Remote control detonators ensured that the car would explode, but I had to be within range of the car when I flipped the switch. One has to be within six hundred feet of most of the commonly sold detonators, and even then, you can't have any interference or anything blocking the way between you and the target or explosive device. Six hundred feet wasn't much, and it left too much room for error if I got too close or something got in the way, and I missed my detonation window.

Higher tech options, like detonating a cell phone by remote tower signal certainly sounded cool, but then the signal could be triangulated to determine the area of the sender of the explosive signal. I didn't want to be discovered or tracked before I could leave the country or find a safe place to get away. As fascinating as it seemed to turn his own phone against him and make it blow up next to his face, I decided against it.

Old school explosives included sticks of dynamite, nitroglycerin, or blasting caps. Sticks of dynamite could still be found in abandoned mines and sold for the purpose of stump removal or boulder and heavy debris removal. They were not as stable as say, the nitroglycerin, and the nitroglycerin approach was less stable than blasting caps. A bomb made with dynamite would require a timing mechanism, a trigger, and several sticks of dynamite to be effective. That was really risky, especially since it would be difficult to explain to the local cops why I had purchased several sticks of dynamite while living in town and not out on a farm in the country or on the side of a mountain. Too bad we had sold the family farm years ago, or this might have been the perfect cover for owning dynamite.

Nitroglycerin as an explosive was surprisingly easier in terms of acquisition, stability, and approach. It was used as heart medicine in pill form, and the liquid form was frequently purchased by hospitals for medical use. However, these medicinal uses were typically diluted because nitroglycerin in its purest form could explode with just a simple bump and jolt.

I could get a few bottles from the hospital to create a bomb. It would explode the minute it made contact with diatomaceous earth and a heat source or a violent impact. In short, I could purchase the diatomaceous earth from a hardware store, sprinkle it on his porch, and use some sort of device to launch the nitroglycerin bottles onto the porch where the diatomaceous earth was sprinkled. I wasn't sure if the big boom I would need would be too little or too much if I used one bag of diatomaceous earth and two bottles of medical nitroglycerin liquid. I wasn't a chemist; I just knew that this would produce a very explosive mess that may or may not set fire to his apartment. It would certainly block the means of his escape, since that one door was the only exit he had on the second story without flinging himself out a window. It would also have to be done at night or during the day when all the neighbors were gone.

It was possible to just set the bottles on his porch in a soft pile of the diatomaceous earth and then fire a flaming arrow at them from afar. In fact, that could be done at night under the cover of darkness. I was an excellent shot with a bow and arrow. I could even use an exploding arrow much like the ones military personnel used. Both would be effective at getting the nitroglycerin and diatomaceous earth to explode like fireworks. In fact, if I carried it through on the 4th of July, everyone would think that the fire and explosion that resulted were caused by stray fireworks. Fireworks were frequently set off at the park two blocks down, and enough illegal fireworks were set off on that street every year. I set this plot on the back burner with a few others that seemed doable.

Blasting caps were the most recent means of exploding something. They were much safer and far more stable than any other explosive. The trouble was these were harder to come by. Since they fell under the classification of "detonators" they were not accessible to just anyone. The kind I thought would be most effective in blowing up my ex was the type that only required a small shaking shock to get them to activate themselves. These would be perfect attached to a wheel on his car or motorcycle since the first pothole or bump in the road he hit would cause the blasting caps to explode.

Buying blasting caps was easier if I could find a farmer's co-op that sold them. I would have to prove that I was a farmer or convince a farming friend to get them for me. None of that would be easy, and with the destruction of my ex-husband, I would have a witness who would be able to tell investigators who killed the bastard. A few companies online sold blasting caps of all types, but you had to ask for a quote for specific types of blasting caps. Doing so would immediately trigger a virtual paper trail right back to my front door. Ergo, blasting caps in the type and number I would need were ruled out.

Fertilizer made for a good bomb too. Extra smelly and quite lethal, ammonium nitrate was widely available and cheap. Some of the most devastating domestic terrorist bombings utilized this fertilizer, so I knew it was quite effective. Yet, all I wanted to do was eliminate one useless person, not dozens or hundreds. It also meant having to get extra components to help the fertilizer ignite and explode. Some of those components were easier to get than others.

There was always the possibility of combining explosive ingredients and components to do the job, but I would have to design the full device and method on my own. Stockpiling items I could get my hands on would trigger a series of alarms as each of these items came into my possession or disappeared from medical storerooms and hardware stores. If I really was going to blow him to kingdom come, I had to be very crafty with the custom bomb design and very wily in my accumulation of its parts. I just wanted something much simpler than that, and death by explosion or explosives didn't seem to be the right thing for a simple elimination. It was just too messy, like guns.

Chapter 13: Death by Torture

How many dozens of soldiers and spies die at the hands of torturers every year? It wasn't a fact I could research since the internet does limit the release of information on torture victims. Considering how often my ex tortured me with gaslighting, verbal assaults on my character, threats of physical harm, emotional abuse, psychological manipulation, and isolation, torture was such an ideal option for death for him. I really felt like he should get a taste of his own medicine, but a dozen times worse.

When I was younger, I remember visiting torture chambers and museums with torture exhibits. They fascinated me because I couldn't imagine the horrific pain of the victims exposed to these devices or their ultimate expiration at the hands of their torturers. My ex and I had even toured a tourist attraction that had involved torture devices when we were on honeymoon. When he sat in an ancient electric chair or slipped himself into the stocks, I mused that those devices looked very appropriate for him. Little did I know that just a week later I would be wishing that he had been left in those torture chamber devices.

You see, when we came back from our honeymoon, I had a message on the voicemail. The phone company was threatening to disconnect service unless we paid up. I was dumbstruck because we had paid all the bills with our wedding gift money before we left, which left us with no money for spending while we were on our trip. That is how bad our financial situation was with his flagrant spending; we were in the hole before we even married.

So, the following day I called the phone company. They informed me that someone had made over $350 of phone calls to a 1-900-HotSexNow number. I was absolutely stunned and floored. I asked when the calls were charged or made. The operator on the line informed me that the calls had been made and charged to our phone on the Saturday following the very day we had married. It meant that while I was busy carving out a paycheck, my brand-new husband was busy spending it on expensive phone sex.

I was so livid that I put a passcode on the phone line so that he could never do that again. He tried one more time in my absence, and the calls were blocked. He was so furious with me when he found out that he threatened me with physical violence unless I gave him the passcode. I refused. He raised his hand to strike me, and then walked away to smash something of mine. Things got uglier and uglier from there until it reached the very last appearance in divorce court. Well, even then it didn't really stop; he would occasionally find something else to use to torture me with, and I would have to threaten or use legal force to stop him.

That wasn't the only incident either. When we found out we were pregnant with our first child, I had hidden a separate checking account with the intent to leave him. He wanted to spend even more money and went digging around to find out why I wasn't putting enough money in our joint account for him to spend. He found where I had hidden the checkbook for the secret account. We had a nasty fight about trust, how I should just trust him, and how I (not him) would end up ruining the marriage because I refused to trust him with all of the money. I knew he was wrong, so I argued. I told him I was tired of the money vanishing before we could pay rent and bills. I was tired of his two-pack-a-day cigarette habit. He claimed he was fed up with the dollar a day I spend on a chocolate bar and that my fat ass didn't need it. Never mind that I was four months pregnant and that I should be allowed to eat what I wanted.

It finally boiled down to him threatening to leave. I was totally okay with that since I was planning on leaving him anyway. He wanted, nay, *insisted* I stay and continue the fight with him even though I was already five minutes late for work. Work was three blocks away from our apartment then, and I wouldn't stay and continue fighting about this. He informed me that I would return to an empty apartment in the morning. (I worked third shift all night.) I shrugged my shoulders, put on the navy surplus peacoat that had once been his and I had claimed for myself for months now, and left.

I walked to work in the middle of that cold February late at night. I was nearly to work when I heard footsteps coming up behind me. They were urgent, and I began to walk faster, terrified that I or the unborn child would be hurt or knocked to the cold and icy cement. Instead, what came after us was worse.

It was him. My "charming" husband of five months, and I had no idea what he wanted. He was still raging, still furious that I had refused to miss work and continue a ridiculous fight when I had patients and responsibilities. He grabbed my left arm and spun me around to face him.

He screamed at me on the sidewalk, demanding I give him the coat I was wearing. When I asked why, he said it was his and it was going with him. He said I had no right to it, and he was demanding I take it off right there in the freezing cold. I was pregnant, and he expected me to go without a coat in the middle of winter. I was appalled. I didn't know what else to do, so I gave him the coat. I walked the rest of the way to work without so much as a scarf to keep my head warm.

When I got to work, I realized that my work badge and keys were in the pocket of the coat. I couldn't enter the building. I didn't' have a phone or a way into the nurse's station. They didn't have a way to page another nurse then unless you had a phone. I couldn't turn around and go back to an apartment with an insane and enraged husband, so I had to find another way into the office. Fortunately, some patients were still awake and mobile. One let me in the door and let me call the charge nurse to get a spare office key.

The next morning, I walked my pregnant self back home again. He had gone so far as to pack suitcases and put them by the front door. Sadly, he didn't leave, but decided he would continue to have a verbal fight with a very tired and very pregnant woman who only wanted to go to bed for the day. It's how he wore me down lots of times, and how he continued to push what he wanted to get his way. He used basic methods of torture, and those basic methods work if the victim is too tired to fight and/or has a lot to lose.

That's why at this very moment torture appealed to me as a form of execution. He should be tortured in all the ways he had tortured me, or worse. I remembered many of the devices used in the Middle Ages, and even some more modern forms of torture.

The rack stretched a human torso and limbs until they were dislocated and broken. I had felt that way sometimes under his browbeating. I felt as though he had pulled every major joint out of place in my body, and I felt broken. I cried thinking about this, but I knew I could not build or buy a rack torture device for the express purpose of making him feel the physical equivalent to the emotional and psychological pain he had put me through.

Tying him to a chair or handcuffing him and then attaching a car battery with cables to his nipples or testicles would be painful, but not enough to kill him. He would find a way to get away from that, and possibly turn it on me.

A device called "the pear" is inserted into orifices in the body and slowly screwed open to force stretch the orifice. It is the torture device upon which the gynecological speculum is designed. The original torture device is shaped literally like a pear and rips open the anus and rectum when fully expanded. For women, this torture device was far worse, since it could be inserted in one additional area of the body. For my ex, this device would probably not be painful or lethal enough, and he would probably enjoy it. I won't get into why.

The "heretic's fork" involved a piece of metal that had two very sharp points on each end. A strap of leather around the double fork tied it around the neck of the victim. One end would pierce the top of the chest and the other the underside of the chin *if* the victim dropped his head below the revered position of "looking to God." Subsequently the device would cause incredible blood loss when the victim would become so fatigued with keeping his head up toward Heaven. Also an effective means of death for someone like my ex who constantly lied about everything even when there was no reason to lie at all.

The "Judas Cradle" caused extensive blood loss from the anus or perineum when victims were suspended above a pyramid-shaped piece of metal atop four legs. Torturers would literally release and drop victims' bottoms onto the pointed end of the pyramid causing irreparable injury. It was used for those accused of adultery and buggery (homosexuality). Again, given the unfaithfulness of my ex-husband, this was a suitable form of torture.

The Chinese water torture was ancient. Like modern day waterboarding, it involved water. Unlike waterboarding, it was a steady drip-drip-drip of water on the victim's forehead making it impossible for him to sleep or rest. Most went mad, but none would die of it, so that ruled out this torture method. It might be fun just to make him feel how crazy he made me feel every time he gaslighted me, but I really wasn't interested in playing a cat and mouse game with him.

Unlike the Chinese water torture, modern waterboarding could kill you. The constant wet cloth over your face with buckets and buckets of water emptied over it could cause you to drown. In fact, less than two inches of water is enough to make anyone drown, so a constant flow of water over your face can kill you. The fact that I wouldn't have to look at his ugly face during waterboarding also appealed to me. However, it would require subduing him, tying him tightly to a board or other flat surface, and then drowning out yelling and screaming meant that it would have to be done somewhere where no one could hear him. That was too much work and too much planning.

The method has to be simpler than that, or at least not involve quite so much blood and yelling. Radio waves and microwaves were modern forms of torture. These waves could cook him from the inside out, but as a form of death-torture, they put me in danger too. Ultimately, I decided that death-torture was only a last-minute execution if nothing else presented itself as a reasonable plan of action.

Chapter 14: Death by Freezing

He could be so cold sometimes; so heartless, so cruel. He feigned kindness in only the way a psychopath could. His body language would give him away, though, and then I would know in those moments he was faking it.

At one point, we were pregnant with our second child. He was not thrilled in the least. He had demanded that we never have any more children. He had his son to continue the family line, and he didn't want any more kids. I firmly told him it wasn't up to him, and he couldn't stop children from happening unless he wanted to stop certain other activities. I suppose I would have been fine with him never touching me ever again, but I did want more children.

My time was running out, and I knew it. My biological clock had been screaming at me for a decade already. There were genetic factors at play. So, when we found out I was pregnant a second time, I was over the moon. He was not.

He was spiteful, angry, and twisted in his treatment of me. He distanced himself as much as he could. He still came with me to the first ultrasound but stood some distance away from the exam table. When the technician couldn't find a heartbeat for the baby, his countenance changed. He moved in, tried to take my hand, pretend he felt bad about the dead child inside me. I knew it was all a lie; a show for the technician who was trying to be consoling.

He went to work. I went home to cry. Three weeks went by before my body finally relinquished "the products of conception". It was two days before Thanksgiving. Guess who was really thankful that year?

While I was dealing with the miscarriage, he tried to play the role of the supportive spouse. Asked if I needed anything. Went to the store to get maxi-pads. Called from the store to ask what kind. If he really knew me, he would have known this tiny detail, wouldn't he?

It didn't matter. He couldn't conceal his joy. He grinned at every turn. Part of me suspected that he might have had something to do with the death of the child. Condom lubricants and drugs like Misoprostol could cause death to a fetus or embryo. The baby had been seven and half weeks along, just about the time I had felt sick and congested and he had handed me something to treat symptoms. I put it out of my head because nobody wants to think that their spouse could be that evil and self-serving. Yet, I had seen such actions in other areas of our lives together, so I couldn't dismiss it entirely.

As a nurse, I was told that women needed time for their bodies to re-regulate and that conception was not entirely possible so soon after a miscarriage. Imagine my surprise when I found myself pregnant less than three months later. I was hopeful and excited then, but he returned to a foul mood, more foul than the last time.

It was at this time that I had slowly started the process of divorce behind the scenes. I found someone to help me draw up the papers. I borrowed the money in secret so he wouldn't notice that my pay was a little short and that he didn't and couldn't spend everything I was supposed to bring home. By the time I found out that this new pregnancy was viable, I was ready to leave.

I spent month after agonizing month being threatened, told I was a whore and a slut, told that this new baby wasn't his, told that he wanted an amniocentesis and a paternity test because he wouldn't pay child support for this one. None of that was true, of course. It was just how he chose to beat me down and run from responsibility. Crush me some more to see me hovel and grovel under his heel, but I had had enough.

He was often chilly and nasty, even to our son now. The little toddler boy was confused. He didn't talk, but I could see his face and how he seemed to wonder why mommy would leave him with daddy sometimes and not come back for hours. (I was working and there was no one else to care for him.) His father would ignore the boy's needs and park him in front of a TV.

At one point I got a call at work. A neighbor had banged on the door until the soon-to-be-ex answered. The neighbor had found our toddler wandering the parking lot in the midst of a dangerous thunderstorm. My charming husband had been sleeping and had ignored my prompts to get up and look after our son because I had to go to work. My gut told me not to leave because my son was clever enough to open doors and go outside. I felt sick when his father told me what had happened. I prayed nothing else untoward had happened to our son in the forty-five minutes I had left him with his father.

This level of coldness that was bent and intent on hurting us, punishing us for everything my ex didn't want and wouldn't involve himself in was exactly what prompted me to imagine a frozen death. When you freeze to death, every cell in your body is momentarily exploded right at the moment of becoming frozen. It starts out as an incredibly painful way to die, until your nerves have frozen, and pain is no longer a signal to your brain. Everything becomes numb and devoid of feeling, much like my ex's actions toward me and the children at times.

There were a couple of ways to freeze him to death. One or two might be easier than the others. Tossing him into a snowbank after delivering a tranquilizer into him on the most rigidly cold day of winter was one way.

Placing him in a freezer chest with a lock on it was another. I had such a freezer chest on the back porch. I kept it plugged in all the time, but rarely kept any amount of food in it. Nobody went to that area of the house, not even me. I would still have to lock it to keep him from escaping, unless I doped him with enough sedative that he would never wake up while he slowly froze to death. The "nice" thing about the freezer chest idea was that he was so short I wouldn't have to chop him up or try to fold him in half to make him fit.

Another way was to shove him out of a plane high enough in the air, specifically over some snow-covered mountains. That wasn't likely despite the fact that we had talked about skydiving lessons many times over when we had been dating. At least shoving him out of the plane would result in either death by rigid cold in the upper atmosphere or death by landing on a mountaintop.

Tying him to a board and leaving him where avalanches were common certainly had its appeal. If he yelled for help, the avalanche he started would be his own doing. It would be difficult to convince him to go on a ski trip with the children and I once they were old enough because he wasn't the downhill skiing type. Some deaths by freezing were person-specific; they had to fit with something that person ordinarily would do for enjoyment or plotting such a death wouldn't work at all.

I imagined finding a way to coax him into a meat locker or a walk-in commercial freezer that locked for the night. It would only take between four and six hours for him to freeze to death inside a walk-in or meat locker but getting him to walk into one was absurd. It's not as though my family owned a restaurant or butcher shop where walking into one of these commercial appliances would be a normal everyday occurrence.

A more probable frozen death was ice fishing. Where we lived, ice fishing was practically ritualistic in winter. He loved to fish; it might have been the only thing that kept him away from the children and I for more than a day. I just had to convince him to try ice fishing, and then shove him into the empty hole in the ice after the ice shanty was propped over the top. The current in the lake under the ice would take him the rest of the way, and the lake patrol and rescue teams would call it an accident. He might fight to regain footing in the shanty, but I'd back off as much as I could and let him flop and flounder while trying to grab at the edge of the ice hole. Lots of people died this way every winter but it never stopped anyone from going ice fishing.

It would require an ice shanty, though. I didn't own one, and most people I knew just rented them. I might be able to convince someone to let us borrow their shanty and ice fishing hole for a day. A hundred bucks would be enough to convince anyone on that frozen lake to go for beer in town and then it would be killing time, literally.

Frozen tanker cars on trains and frozen food trucks were a couple of other options. However, trying to get a body that wasn't dead yet into a frozen train car or into the back of a frozen food truck that just happened by was both challenging and a rare occurrence. Such tankers and trucks didn't come through town every day.

I suppose there were other ways of freezing someone to death, such as dropping them into a hole in the ground in the middle of nowhere in the middle of winter and hoping his yells for help didn't attract attention. Putting his unconscious self in a cave with no light and no fire in winter might also work, but again, that wasn't very realistic or feasible in terms of where we resided.

If anything, the chest freezer or the ice fishing were probably the best options here. I knew I was still toying with ideas. I wanted the most appropriate, most lethal, and most final death for this monster. Some days I wish I could kill him several times over in multiple fashions, but you only get one chance to kill someone completely. The rest is just overkill. I didn't want this to be a "crime of passion" because I felt no passion for him at all. It had to be a "one and done" scenario that just fit with all of the hell I had been through with him while still being appropriate for his personality, location, and moral bankruptcy. So far, I had spent about five years just musing on these few things. I suspected it might be another five years or more.

Chapter 15: Secret Assassin Moves Using Common Items to Kill People

Besides finding medieval torture devices fascinating, I often found that spies and the ways in which they were trained to fight and kill people fascinating. Dark, I know, but spies trained to be assassins knew stuff no one else on earth could know. These quiet, secret ways were so deadly that it was rare for any former spy to release that information to anyone that hadn't been in service to God and country.

Quiet and secret; I always felt like I was doing this little dance with my former spouse. I'd run and hide, duck and cover, bury things I didn't want him to know, find or see. Many women in abusive relationships have to do this to protect themselves on some level. I hid money, ferreted it away little bit by little bit to help finance my exit from a bad decision. I would hide feelings and thoughts too; they were not private anymore and he would find a way to force them into the open and use my words to assault me. I couldn't keep a diary, talk to friends, or email anyone without being tracked, berated, and dehumanized in an attempt to dominate and control me.

He would do a different dance. Similar to espionage, he'd look for anything I was hiding, covering up, trying to keep out of his hands. Sometimes he would twist things I said or did to fit his narrative and then use his narrative to manipulate me or prevent me from gaining the upper hand. I was in psychological hell all the time, worried about what would come next. At other times, nothing would happen, and I'd be terrified that his silence was the actual punishment.

These are the same mind games spies play, so why not use the same secret methods of death on him? There were some especially useful methods that were so simple, so easy, one might even refer to them as a form of "invisible death." When I first heard or read about these methods, I had hoped to learn them with great skill, but managing to execute them with the precision of a well-trained spy may have been purely conjecture. It was impossible to predict if I would have done these correctly, and certainly no other person I knew would submit themselves to a "spy's death" for me to see if I had it right.

One such method involved a rolled newspaper. A tightly rolled newspaper comprised of 25 sheets overlapping and bent in half after rolling it created an amazingly strong weapon. Spies would deliver a death blow to the throat right under the chin or use the bend middle edge to crack a skull like a peanut shell. The best part is that the paper could be burned, tossed to the wind, separated and disseminated into a dozen or more trash bins, etc. A basic newspaper purchased at a news stand could do all that.

Another method was to deliver a blow to the bottom of the victim's nose using the heel of my hand. The meaty part of the palm with the fingers spread was all you needed. I knew you had to put your full weight and full upward thrust force into the movement. The successful action essentially breaks the person's nose and shoves the bones into his brain causing instant brain death from a bleed that doesn't stop. I didn't know if I had enough full body strength and forward momentum to execute this correctly.

A piano wire or wire cutter from pottery or a cheese slicing wire was another lethal spy move. These wires are very strong, sharp, and thin. Pulled taut over a throat they can take a person's head off if you want to take it that far. Unfortunately, I had already ruled out using any method that was particularly bloody and messy, since cleaning myself up afterwards would leave too much trace evidence.

The same held true for a pencil or fountain pen. Both could be dangerous stabbing weapons but pulling them free to allow him to bleed to death still left a mess and the possibility he might get help before actually dying. I could burn the pencil, but the pen was another matter. The fountain pen might also be used to deliver an injection of some type of poison, but there was still the stabbing and bleeding aspects I didn't want to deal with.

A chair commonly used in every kitchen, or a short bar stool found in every bar could knock him out and then be used to strangle him. The lower legs are used to straddle the neck and crush the windpipe, but I didn't want to be caught. Choking always leaves enough evidence in and on a corpse for a pathologist to figure out what happened.

Forks, knives and even spoons can kill, but they are "stabby" objects too. Bludgeoning with pickle jars or small kitchen appliances leave telltale marks, even though they are quite effective as well. Killing with stilettos and belts also leave marks, so those items were crossed off my list. In fact, any common item I could use like a spy to kill that required use as a stabbing object was out, as was anything that would leave an obvious and unique mark.

I heard of a nurse once that had been prosecuted for abusing patients. She had used a man's gym sock filled with quarters or metal padlocks to deliver insane blows to the head and torso. She had been fired and disallowed to practice nursing ever again, which was good. Her methods had not been discovered by the very mild bruises left behind by her vicious beatings, but by another nurse who had witnessed an attack. It seems that coins or padlocks in socks barely leave a mark, which is why none of the other nurses knew or realized that the patients were regularly beaten by this monster.

This method appealed to me, but unfortunately the only way for this to prove deadly was to use it repeatedly on my ex's head. It meant securing him to a chair and keeping him quiet while I repeatedly struck him with the concealed metal objects in a sock. The objects in the sock could be soaked in peroxide and washed with soap after the fact, and the sock could be burned. I wasn't comfortable with this bizarre bludgeoning method, no matter how well it might have worked. There were too many unknown variables involved, including how many blows it would take and how long I could detain him tied to a chair.

Another common approach to killing someone with everyday objects was strangulation. Spies would use scarves, shirts, pants, and anything else that had long enough parts to twist quickly into a tight "rope" and then strangle someone. Virtually any clothing object that didn't stretch excessively could work, and then the item could be burned, given away to a thrift store to some unsuspecting thrift store customer, or washed and neatly restored to the spot where I got it from. The more I could hide the weapon in plain sight, the more I gravitated toward this idea.

It seemed to tie in so well with how we used to dance around each other, hiding secrets from each other and constantly being distrustful. No marriage can stand if there is no trust, and we definitely never had an ounce of trust. Maybe it was because he had lied, cheated, and stole from me again and again. Maybe it was because he constantly made me feel like everything that was bad had happened because of *my* actions or reactions to things he did. At one point he even told me flat out that he wouldn't need to treat me so badly if I didn't react to the awful things he did. My head really hurt after that. I really had to convince myself for years after the divorce that I wasn't at fault for most of what had happened. He had really driven that into my head and made me question everything I did for years.

Strangulation using clothes or other cloth items, however, would require enormous amounts of anger and adrenaline. He was short for a guy, but he could pick up my 200-pound self and toss me across a room. With enough of his own adrenaline coursing through his body, there was little chance I would succeed with this approach. He would have to be unconscious first and not wake up when I began to strangle him. Trace fibers on the neck would reveal what clothing or cloth item was used, and I didn't want to leave behind any evidence at all. Yet it was becoming quite clear to me that the only way any of this was going to work was to subdue him first. I might have to break my plan up into a couple of different parts; subdue and then kill.

Chapter 16: Death by Forced Gluttony

There's something to be said about a person that uses others to force them to give up everything for just that one person. It's not just a form of greed; it's a form of gluttony. When money and food and sex and dominance and acquisition are everything to the abusive partner, there's nothing he or she won't do to get whatever he or she wants a lot of.

That was certainly true in my marriage. Money was a big driving force. Many times, he would sit back and not work at all, forcing me to work double shifts all the time. He would have that money spent before it ever hit our shared bank account. If there wasn't enough, wasn't *more*, I got the ugly end of it.

I can recall while we were still dating that he had remarked how he had "always wanted to be involved with a sugar mama." I looked at him askance and informed him I wasn't a sugar mama, and I never would be. He laughed. I should have paid attention to that laugh, as it was actually a warning for his expectations of me in this relationship.

When it came to sex, there was either an insatiable appetite, or a non-existent appetite. I really couldn't stand either. I didn't want to be in bed with him at all when he was insistent that I stay there at the ready for him like some sex toy or blow-up doll. I didn't want to be around him when he constantly ignored me either because it meant that he was running around with someone else. I knew his mental health was the reason for these behaviors, but I finally stopped excusing the behaviors when it became clear that he didn't care if he caused me injury or death as a result of his actions. He only cared about his own greed and his own gluttony.

If it wasn't money or sex, it was food. He would go days without eating, like some camel that didn't need to eat. It's how I realized that starvation would never work on him as a kill method. He'd just ignore what his body said and put his mind and focus elsewhere. When he wasn't ignoring his own hunger pains, he'd sit and eat like King Henry VIII. Four chicken sandwiches, three double cheeseburgers, a fry and a large cola. Six pieces of fried chicken and biscuits. A dozen tacos followed by refried beans and red beans and rice with an extra-large drink; it was astounding to see him eat and never gain much weight. I eventually realized that he didn't gain weight because he had such long stretches of not eating interspersed with eating huge, gut-bursting meals.

Constantly acquiring everything related to a particular hobby was a never-ending theme with him too. One year I had to surrender any claim to a tax refund because he wanted to spend the entire refund on photography equipment. Massive telephoto lenses and a digital camera worth over a grand; these items along with backdrops and lighting and reflectors absorbed every penny and then some. Another year all the money went to buy catfishing poles commonly used to fish for giant catfish in the Mississippi. The poles ended up in the garage until I sold them later on when he left the children and I for one of his whores. The camera equipment went to a pawn shop when we couldn't pay rent because he had spent all the money again. Any time he became interested in a hobby, it was all or nothing, and after a few months he would grow bored with it and sell it off to a pawn shop. The only things he ever kept were guns, and that worried me immensely.

Considering the non-stop gluttony and greed, I began to think how people could die that way. Gluttony and greed were two of the seven deadly sins. They had been portrayed in many movies. Those that succumbed to them in the penultimate moment before true death met with most unpleasant ends.

I could force-feed him until his stomach exploded. It was gruesome, but I never had to see what happened to his guts internally. I would only know that force-feeding him had worked. I could tie him to a chair, put a tube down his throat into his esophagus, and pour liquids and liquid nutrition down the tube until it killed him. I could puree food or use baby food to expand the stomach to the point of bursting. I could hold a gun on him and force him to eat far past the point of fullness.

All of these were possible, but which was *probable*? He wasn't overweight or obese; he could get up from the table any time and force me to use the gun. As a nurse I knew how to put in a nasogastric tube or an esophageal feeding tube, but that knowledge would make it clear to the police that only someone medically trained to do that could be responsible. They would check my background and my employment history, and I would be suspect #1 ten times over. I could secure him to the chair and pinch his nose shut, forcing him to open is mouth to breath and force the liquids and soft foods in again and again.

That last option was almost viable. The nose would have to be thoroughly closed somehow. I could stitch it shut while he was in the chair, but it would have to look quite sloppy, amateurish and unprofessional to throw off suspicion. Having to breathe and eat with just one's mouth increased the possibility of death by pneumonia or death by aspiration of food too. The biggest problem was the amount of time it would take to complete the job.

The human stomach can expand to hold up to one quart of liquid and masticated food. That was 32 ounces of food bits and liquids or 32 ounces of just liquids. I would have to force-feed him three or four times that to make his stomach burst and feed him an anti-emetic pill to avoid vomiting. The anti-emetic was key to keeping everything in his stomach and forcing it to accept and expand beyond its natural ability to hold edible contents. It meant tying him to a chair, forcing him to take the anti-emetic thirty minutes before the force-feeding, and then push as much into his gullet as I could with his nose sealed shut. He could still yell and scream.

An esophageal tube would prevent yelling and screaming, but it would give me and my profession away. I would need at least three hours for this ordeal and every step would have to be perfect and not interrupted by any outside distraction. The nasogastric tube would leave less of a trace in his esophagus than the esophageal tube, but it wouldn't prevent him from yelling and screaming.

Force-feeding was the perfect form of death for such a gluttonous, all-consuming, greedy and destructive pig like my ex. Yet, the way to force-feed him was not something anyone could perfect unless walls were sound-proof, and I didn't have to be anywhere else taking care of anyone else. As appropriate as I might have seen this form of death, it would be too obvious as a murder scene to the cops because nobody force-feeds themselves a ton of liquids, baby food, pureed food, or anti-emetics to keep from throwing up.

I would just have to allow myself to imagine what it would be like to send the greedy bastard out this way rather than actually execute him with this approach.

Chapter 17: Death by Electrocution or Bioelectric Disruption

Sometimes children and teenagers do things for shock value. They love seeing the expression on adults' faces when they say or do something completely unexpected and perhaps unacceptable to the adults in the room. I remember doing this often as a teenager, and I enjoyed the results because I had spent so many of my years being the perfectly well-behaved child and I was tired of it. My friends, if they were around, encouraged it by laughing at the things I said or did that caused adults to gasp and have that look of utter shock on their faces.

I wonder what they would think now if they knew I was planning the perfect murder. It's such a far cry from that young girl who was kind to everyone and had no idea of the misery adult life would bring her. Some tiny corner of my heart missed that young girl and all of her hopes, dreams, ambitions and goals for the rest of her life. I wish I could go back in time and warn her and tell her not to pursue anything else but what she was good at and what she loved most in life. I wanted to warn her to avoid some of the worst mistakes in her life and run from those mistakes just as fast as she could. I knew I couldn't do that and that I couldn't protect that younger version of me from the present day I have. It didn't stop me from wishing I could.

My ex-husband, on the other hand, seemed to have never left that teenage moment where shock and awe were valuable. He had never grown up. He never got past whatever age he really was, and the desire to continually shock others to get a reaction was a daily thing. It could get a little obnoxious when he said or did something in an attempt to be funny or get his kicks more than once in a day, but I tried to ignore that when we were married. I realized that I only had to leave the apartment or leave the room to ignore him until I could tolerate his immature behavior for another few hours.

Unfortunately, that immature behavior only grew and became worse after marriage, as most things do when you can't get away from somebody and you realize you're tired of it already. The behavior also became darker and more menacing rather than intentionally and stupidly lighthearted. Maybe it was because I had certain expectations and ideas about marriage, and I was annoyed that those expectations fully missed the mark once married. Maybe it was because I had married someone who had hid most of his true nature and felt he could release the beast now that I couldn't shake him or tell him to get out. Whatever the cause or reason, the shocks delivered were another means by which he would attempt to break me emotionally and psychologically.

Shortly after we were engaged and just before the wedding, we had been sitting on the couch and he had said something that was both shocking and stupid in an attempt at humor. It was also a little insulting. He got the shock response from me he was looking for, and a playful slap on his upper arm. Instead of continuing to laugh, his countenance quickly changed. It was a night and day switch, from mirth to black storm clouds in seconds.

"Don't you EVER do that again!" he growled low and fierce.

I was taken aback, and I thought he was joking again so I laughed. His face did not change, and his jaw was locked with obviously stiff muscles raising through the flesh. I had to look at him with a puzzled look for a moment before responding.

"Don't do what? Laugh?" I asked.

"No, hit me. Don't ever hit me again or I'll call the cops on you."

I was floored. He was serious.

"Are you serious? I'm not hitting you. That was a playful slap and nothing else."

"No, you hit me, and I won't allow you to hit me ever."

The playful slap was nothing. It was of the same lightness that my friends and I had lightly slapped each other for saying silly or funny things our whole lives. We never hit to hurt, which is how I knew now that this wasn't an actual hard slap on his arm.

But he was really serious. He would actually call the cops on his fiancé for a playful slap. Little did I know that he was setting the stage for making me feel crazy for accusing him of physical harm and physical threats, which he did do once we were married. He never struck me, but the threats and being cornered and having him scream an inch from my face was as shocking and terrifying as this one revealing moment of mirth turned darkness on the couch.

A lot of the behavior and threats that came later were a sort of shock and awe tactic, but they were no longer playful. They were volatile, hostile, threatening, and manipulative. If I allowed my face to show fear or shock or terror, he would back off and go into another room of the apartment and yell from there. If I refused to look shocked or terrified, the close encounter and threatening behavior continued until I gave him the satisfaction of the facial expression he wanted. I eventually decided not to show any emotion during these episodes, choosing to attempt to risk physical harm and possibly decrease the behavior through ignoring and extinguishing the behavior over time.

That's the problem with attempting to terrorize someone and dominate and attempt to control someone who is more successful and smarter than you. That smarter person will figure out how to avoid you and turn things upside down to get an attacker or abuser to stop. I was the smarter person, and I knew it. He was in a state of arrested development where he had learned to use these behaviors on others to get what he wanted. I had a degree in human psychology and development, and it certainly helped me figure out how to survive his "fits."

I can remember watching a movie where patients in an asylum in the '60's were treated with electroshock therapy. It altered their brain chemistry for a noticeably short time, or so it was supposed. Patients seemed to do better, albeit they regularly became drooling, staring shells of their former selves. I thought about how my husband at the time could have benefited from this type of therapy, although electroshock therapy was rarely used anymore. A patient had to be the most violent and incurable individual there was before this type of therapy would even be considered.

Yet, what if I dosed my husband with just a little bit of electricity at a time? It wouldn't be difficult since he was frequently tinkering with electronics. All I would have to do is plug a computer or other device back into the wall when he wasn't looking, and bare wires were exposed. Those tiny little wires inside these machines couldn't possibly deliver the kind of voltage someone would receive in a mental health facility. If he were able to let go of the bare wires quick enough, it really wouldn't do much at all.

The thought culminated into something else as the years went by. The various ways in which one could electrocute somebody were portrayed on TV, but I knew that not all electrocutions dramatized for television would legitimately and effectively kill a person. The idea that a toaster plugged into the wall could kill you in a bathtub was only partly true. The toaster would have to operate at higher wattages or volts than most other toasters to be a murder weapon, and you couldn't make it look like an accident because nobody makes toast in the bathroom. It also wouldn't work because my ex didn't eat toast, or breakfast, or take baths. It wouldn't have the same effect in a shower as it would in a bathtub full of water.

The same held true for a hair dryer. He didn't use one, and he would have to have cause to use one while showering, which he didn't. Hair dryers had the right amount of electrical supply for electrocution, but it didn't suit him to use one.

I could set various electrical traps that would cause electrocution and look like accidents, but when our son came along and then our daughter, those intended accidents could have killed them. I couldn't make lightning strike his car, his boat, or his motorcycle, much less manufacture enough "lightning" to make that a reasonable cause of death. I could create electrical short circuits in the dashboards of the vehicles he drove by himself, but it would require teaching myself how to rewire some of the electrical parts in the vehicles and making it look purely accidental. To be purely accidental, I would have to choose the one thing he drove the most or choose the boat since the water would act as a massive conductor to jolt his body into eternal repose.

I wasn't an electrician. I was a nurse. I turned my attention to the arrest of bioelectric impulses created within the human body. The bioelectricity the human body produces is meant to keep the heart pumping, the brain receiving and sending signals to nerves and muscles and get muscles to respond to requests to move a certain way. Disrupt the body's own electrical impulses, and you disrupt life. It's why electrical current outside the body and bioelectrical current don't mix.

There were methods I could use to disrupt his bioelectric signals to his heart and his brain. A defibrillator was one such machine. When used on someone whose heart is fully functional, it disrupts the heart's ability to regulate its own electrical signals. By disrupting the heart's signals, the heart actually *stops* when a defibrillator is used on a healthy (or reasonably healthy) heart. Portable defibrillators were now sold to anyone, and we could buy one and keep it in the trunk of the car. I could easily argue that it was for emergency use only if I came upon an accident scene where someone's heart had stopped.

I could use the defibrillator on him as he slept. I could sneak into his apartment at night when he was asleep and give him the heart-stopping jolt. The problem was is that he would have to remain in cardiac arrest. His heart might restart itself; that happens sometimes.

I could jolt his brain instead. The defibrillator pads placed at the base of his skull would deliver electrical current to his central nervous system and interrupt all signals traveling from the brain to every last area of the body. The defibrillator would have to be cranked to maximum to attempt this just once. Once was all I got if I was going to sneak into his apartment late at night.

A cattle prod or a stun gun could accomplish something similar. In fact, a cattle prod inserted into the mouth or rectum would deliver current even faster because of the wet interior surfaces of these areas of the body. I wasn't likely to get close enough to him to make that happen, but maybe placing his hand in water while he slept or soaking him and hitting him with the volts would work. Women were buying stun guns for protection all the time. There were no rules on buying a cattle prod from a reliable resource either.

There was also the possibility of an S&M "play kit" I could get. You hook the tiny jumper cable clips to the human anatomy as you choose, and the other ends connect to a car battery. As I understood it, it delivered one hell of a punch, but no one had ever died from it unless they had a weak heart or a congenital defect of the pulmonary system. I couldn't imagine getting close enough to my ex again to even consider this, so I went back to the more likely ideas. Those ideas still required me getting within a foot of him, or six feet with the stun gun.

I didn't think I could do that. However, he would certainly get the shock of his life, perhaps the shock and awe he was deserving and always trying to squeeze from others. Imagine his surprise when he looked up and saw that it was me, jolting him a good one. It was at that very moment that I realized that a little bit of that young girl who loved shock and awe was still alive and well within me, but that she shouldn't be let out to do this one thing. Otherwise, she and I would be no better and no more mature for it.

Chapter 18: Death by Solvents and Acids

There are so many horror movies, TV plot twists, and real-life crime stories where someone is dropped in a vat of chemicals or splashed with a bucket of acid. As awful as it seems, one has to question if it's really possible to kill someone this way. Maybe all you do is severely disfigure the person and cause them untold pain and suffering for life. That could be worse than death itself.

Psychological pain is a lot like that. It stays with you for years and years. It haunts you in your sleep, if you can sleep, and someday it may just ebb away just enough for you to relax and breathe the smallest bit. That isn't quite the case with people who suffer post-traumatic stress disorder, and I was certain that PTSD was exactly what I had.

While I'm sure that PTSD is far worse for people who have actually been assaulted or physically harmed over and over again, the psychological aspects leave a scar that outlasts the physical marks in your skin. You always jump, always look over your shoulder, react in a hostile manner to protect your feelings of vulnerability and hide your fear, and shrink away from others when they approach you and get too close for your own comfort. It boxes you up in such a way that you almost feel like an imprisoned genie, except that no amount of magic is going to save you or release you from the emotional prison lamp that holds you.

I had my share of counselors, and over the years I made sure that my children had regular and frequent contact with therapists too. I wanted them to know what healthy behavior for people was, and to recognize when their father's behavior was wrong. If my behavior was ever in question, I wanted my children to be able to feel safe to point it out to me or question my behavior without fear of violent reprisal.

I can remember when my children were small and forced to live with their father for a time. It was the worst two years of my life, but I had been cornered and he had used third parties to threaten and abuse me. Nobody gets over that. Every time I heard "social worker" going forward I had a vile taste in my mouth like rotting meat, and I secret desire to slaughter every social worker that dared to cross my path. His lies and actions were bad enough; their ignorance and ugly commentaries were worse. Their profession made my body tense up like a former rape victim's; they needed to leave me and my children alone.

In this particular time in our long and unhappy history, a memory involving our son still makes me cringe. This sweet, rambunctious little boy had been playing near his father's precious computer, the very expensive gaming computer he bought himself after he managed to get the children's disability checks transferred over to him. He had yelled at our son in front of me while I was "allowed" to visit, telling this little boy not to play too close to the computer and the open bottle of Cola next to the computer. I knew what would happen, but I was unable to stop the chain of events that were so easy to predict.

Our son was indeed rambunctious, and he accidentally bumped the desk where this precious piece of gaming tech sat. The Cola bottle tipped over and dumped its contents all over the keyboard. My ex jumped up and grabbed the bottle and set it right, but not before two thirds of its remaining contents coated the keyboard.

The ex lit into a fury, trying to madly dry off the keyboard while simultaneously screaming at our son for doing something that was not only an accident, but also staged by my ex. If he had taken the soda bottle off of the desk or at least had screwed the cap back on, no harm would have come to his precious computer. Our son stood there in shock while his father screamed at him and berated him, telling him what a stupid child he was. The poor boy got over his shock and began to cry, which only made it much worse.

You don't cry in front of someone who will abuse you further for the crying.

Our son reached for me, and I grabbed him, cradling him in my arms, hoping that the violent outburst would be redirected toward me. I knew it well; I could handle it better since I knew how this sort of behavior carried on. I was right; as our son was comforted in my arms for an accident his father staged, my ex's rage turned on me. He berated me for coddling the boy and berated me for comforting him while he cried. I didn't try to reason with him; only mumbled under my breath that it was just a keyboard.

I think my ex heard some of what I had said because his voice pitched upward as he informed me that "it wasn't just any keyboard. These keyboards are EXPENSIVE!" I didn't say another word because at that moment our daughter toddled over to get closer to me and get out of range of her father. She had a blank stare on her face as she looked in his direction. It was all I could do to beg God silently to help me get the kids away from him and back home again where they belonged.

Sometimes I imagine his overreaction to cola on a keyboard. It was like acid thrown in someone's face. Explosive, burning, damaging, but not totally beyond saving. I imagined him being melted by some sort of acid or a solvent. I knew there were some easily accessible chemicals out there that could do just that.

Battery acid, for example, could be harvested from several car batteries. You had to wear protective equipment to keep the tiniest drop of acid from hitting your clothes or skin. That stuff could eat through flesh in minutes, and anyone who had ever been doused with a couple liters of battery acid usually did not survive. It would eat through flesh, muscle, and organ tissue. It could be useful in dissolving a dead body, too, as bones could be dissolved in it. No useful DNA for identifying a body would be left behind.

Battery acid was comprised of sulfuric acid. If enough of it ate through the neck and face, it would damage the trachea and cause the victim to asphyxiate and die. Eating through heart and lungs would also cause death, but it would take a 4- or 5-quart pail of the stuff removed from full car batteries and splashed on the victim's chest or back to be effective. It also doesn't kill immediately. He would have enough time to tell a witness or tell anyone who did this to him. I would be too obvious to anyone on the street when dressed in hazmat gear.

Piranha acid is a nasty cousin to sulfuric acid. Its ingredients are a combination of the battery acid and hydrogen peroxide. It's so dangerous that chemists won't even keep it in labs unless they have to. A nasty chemical reaction works together between these two acidic compounds to dissolve everything it touches. It's essentially akin to humans on crack; the peroxide is the crack that negatively boosts the sulfuric acid to new and very unpleasant heights in terms of destruction and devastation. Because it is easy to get battery acid from a car battery and hydrogen peroxide from the corner drugstore, it's the dangerous substance of nightmares.

I didn't want to stick around and watch his flesh melt off any more than I wanted to hear bloodcurdling screams of pain. I guess even I had my limits where acids were concerned. It is probably why I turned my attention to other chemicals found in a hospital that could be used to either create a solvent or were commonly used in hospital operations as well as used in lots of other commercial locations.

Drain cleaner, for example, is comprised primarily of sodium hydroxide with some alkaline compounds added for quicker activation. They could leave scarring on the skin, but they could also be washed away for minimal damage. The most effective way was to get someone to *swallow* drain cleaner, but there was no way he was going to do that unless he was tied down and force-fed the substance.

Bleach could burn and sting, and it could irritate the sinuses and throat. What was particularly dangerous about bleach in a hospital is that we had to be careful and avoid mixing it with ammonia. These two common hospital cleaners and sanitizers create toxic vapors that arrest the body of oxygen, suffocating the brain, and causing unparalleled damage to the nose, throat, trachea and lungs. Death is imminent if left in an enclosed space with these two chemicals mixed in a bucket.

What most people don't know is that a surplus of ammonia mixed with a lesser amount of bleach also creates boiling reactive chemical that then starts shooting sprays of this dangerous new mixture. Chemical burns to the flesh will never heal, and the areas where this mixture touches are left raw and open. The open wounds can cause someone to bleed to death if the victim isn't removed from the enclosed space and taken to a hospital immediately.

I had access to both bleach and ammonia. So did every other person in the world. The difference was that, as a nurse, I would have been trained not to mix these two cleaning agents. I would know what would happen if mixed. That meant that the police could draw a line straight to me if they dug around long enough.

Other solvents found in paint shops, furniture repair and stripping shops and the like were only lethal if mixed and inhaled. It still meant that he would have to be knocked unconscious and left in a tight space with the gases, vapors, or fumes building to the point where brain death was the result. Benzenes and alkanes were really only the ones I was most familiar with, and chloroform was looking more like the right knock-out drug to use to get close enough to kill him. With the exception of melting him in a barrel or vat of acid, the solvents still had the potential wiggle room for salvation, if someone found my ex in time. Since I didn't have the stomach to melt him, and I didn't have the absolute certainty and guarantee that solvents would permanently end him. I only made note of the chloroform.

Chloroform, while used as a solvent, is also used to temporarily knock people out. We kept some in the hospital as part of a backup system for surgeries and emergencies in the event that we were unable to sedate a patient as a result of lack of functional equipment or lack of other general anesthesia agents.

If left to the open air, people exposed to chloroform regain consciousness, albeit rather slowly. I let the idea of chloroform swim around in my brain for a while, seeing as it was apparent to me that I would have to somehow get very close to my ex to carry out my plan. Whatever my plan was, I think chloroform might play a starring role in it.

Chapter 19: Exsanguination

Being married to someone who is never there for you, never a partner in life, and never particularly helpful or very caring toward you is both draining and defeating. Every new dawn brings a longer day where you know that if something unusual or atypical happens, you don't have someone you can lean on for support. He's just not that into you, nor is he there for anyone else but himself.

That's how I spent every day of every year of my marriage. I'd wake up, groan, and realize that the only person who was going to do anything worthwhile or productive that day was me. I was the only one who was going to get up, finish college, grow babies internally, care for babies externally, and keep house all while making a paycheck. More and more I didn't get excited when I would wake up in the morning. Every morning became drudgery, and every night when I could go to sleep a blessing.

Perhaps the worst moments in all of this were the days when I wasn't feeling well. I was exhausted from trying to meet the demands of new motherhood, overwhelmed by work and school, and desperately needing a break from daily tasks about the apartment. This day, I woke to feeling nauseated and woozy. I wasn't sure why I felt so physically ill; I just did. Maybe I had the flu. Maybe my body was trying to tell me that a break was so necessary that it would force me to take one if I wasn't going to do it of my own volition. Maybe it was because I was six months post-partum and hormone levels were shifting back to normal. Whatever the reason, I didn't feel well at all.

My charming husband was snoring in bed beside me, but our infant son had started crying from the next room. Like most mothers and wives, I rolled over and nudged him hard until he growled at me. I told him I wasn't feeling well; won't he please get up and take care of our baby?

A good husband would understand. A great husband would get up and handle the situation without a moment's hesitation. Not my husband; he wasn't about to let a silly thing like an unwell wife interrupt *his* sleep.

In fact, as our son continued to cry and my head continued to spin and my stomach felt like water swirling around in a toilet bowl. I tried a second time to force him to get up and help. What I got was unexpected and unpleasant.

He rolled over and looked at me.

Then he growled, "Get your fat, lazy ass up and take care of our son! It's YOUR job as his mother to take care of him! I don't give a shit if you're sick or not feeling well! It's YOUR job, not mine!"

I was completely taken aback. What century were we living in? I took a second to think and check myself; no, we were definitely living in the 21st century. How was it then that this meathead laying next to me believed he didn't have any responsibility at all to look after our baby or make an effort to care for his wife who wasn't feeling well and was already carrying the major load of everything else around her?

Rather than incur another round of verbal abuse, I got up. Even with as ill as I felt, my son's adorable little face was a more welcome sight than his asshole father's face in the next room. The little guy needed a diaper change, a feeding, and comfort. He was so sweet; I just hoped I wouldn't need to vomit while caring for him. Luckily for him, something about holding this sweet little baby made me temporarily forget how my head and my gut felt.

What I didn't forget from that day forward was that I would NEVER have an equal partner in anything. The husband (and then the ex) made it perfectly clear that he didn't have to do anything he didn't want to do and that I would be expected to do everything else. He was even clear about the fact that I couldn't have any friends that were male, nor could I ever have an affair, not that I had time for such frivolities anyway. He, on the other hand, deemed it perfectly okay to have lots of female friends, visit ex-girlfriends at will, and converse with any female he wanted. When I called him on the double standard, I was informed that it wasn't a double standard because he "knew he wouldn't really cheat."

As the days dragged on into years, I felt like I had the life-force drained from me. What is life-force, but for blood? Blood is the one thing the body cannot live without. You also cannot live without a brain, although some babies born without a brain somehow manage to live several days or weeks before finally succumbing to death. Blood, however, served as the vehicle to bring life to everything in the body. I felt like I had the blood drained out of me every day and every night as I went to sleep.

I recalled the medieval practice of bloodletting. It was common for centuries to cut the wrists of people who were sick with unknown maladies or those they thought were possessed of demons. Releasing the blood would remove the sickness from the body or trick demons into thinking that their living host was dying and therefore evict the demons from the host. For me to do that to myself would only invite trouble because people would think I was trying to commit suicide. Most bloodletting "patients" of the past often did die because there was so little knowledge as to how much blood the human body held and how much could be released from the body before someone would die.

Yet, I knew exactly how much blood the human body held and how much someone could relinquish and survive. The average human body contains between 9 and 12 pints of blood. A loss of about 40%, or almost half, results in death if blood transfusions aren't immediate. I had seen my fair share of accident patients come into the hospital on the verge of death, consuming whatever blood supply the EMTs had on tap in the ambulance on the way in. Some made it, some didn't.

Exsanguination; that was the term given in the Victorian era for dead people who seemed to have been drained of blood or looked like they had been drained of blood. Back then, they thought a body that completely lacked blood was the result of a vampire, and this dead body needed to be treated for vampirism before it too became a blood-sucking monster. What they didn't know or understand then was that blood carried oxygen throughout the body. A lack of oxygenated blood at death created the deathly pallor of the deceased. Blood generally ceased to move after some time, coagulating in the body as it pooled in blood vessels and organs.

However, there were some legitimate deaths by exsanguination. It is very possible to drain nearly every last drop of blood from the body. The very life-force is emptied and collected into jars and disposed of if the body is already dead. In the case of killing someone, the blood can be collected for the purpose of saving another life.

A new idea formed in my head. I could physically do to my ex what he had done to me emotionally and psychologically for years. I could drain the physical life-giving substance from his body. It actually doesn't take that long if you know exactly where to insert the needle (or needles) and filling blood donation bags made the plan even better.

He would need to be subdued, but I already counted on that because any good idea I had thus far and had shelved for my ex's ultimate demise required sedating him. Then it was a matter of having multiple blood collection kits available to extract his blood. I would only need to extract five or six pints to be lethal. If I wanted to be particularly sadistic, I could take all the pints he had. It might require ten, eleven, or twelve blood collection kits. He was short and paunchy, so I didn't think he would have the most blood possible, but you never know.

To make the job go faster, I could restrain him in a bed covered in plastic sheeting. Then I could set up a collection kit connected to each arm and to each femoral artery. With four kits going at once, it might only take an hour or two to fully drain him of blood. If I put each of the pints of blood on ice in a lunch cooler, I could easily sneak them into the hospital and into the blood storage rooms or into the ambulance blood storage drawers. I knew what my ex's blood type was since he frequently donated his drug-laden and STD-laced plasma for cash. He had told me at one point what blood type he was "in case he was dying and either of the kids were a match."

There's no way I'd ever allow either child to give him one drop of their blood. Thankfully, they weren't matches at all. He'd have to find his blood supply somewhere else. I never told him that because he had always accused me of being "an unfaithful whore" and he didn't know or understand that your offspring may not be blood type matches for you. I didn't need old and false accusations coming up again when he was faced with the stark truth that his children's blood would never save him.

I went back to thinking about how his blood did contain multiple drugs, both legal and illegal, and how that might impact the unknowing recipients of his post-demise "donations". He could be carrying AIDS, HIV, or hepatitis of any type. He certainly had a grand time sleeping around both before and after the divorce. Any of that was possible, and it was also possible that he wouldn't know he was a carrier because he avoided going to a doctor unless he had to.

The drugs in his blood were also a problem. Some might filter out of a healthy person's kidneys quickly, but it was somewhat cruel to subject someone else to that. If the drugs were such that an addict with a problem encountered blood or plasma from my ex's blood with a particular drug in it, it would create quite a reaction, especially if that addict were attempting to come clean and sober. I knew the nicotine levels in his blood may be particularly harmful, given the level of cigarettes and vape smoke he consumed daily.

There was nothing I wanted more than to drain my ex dry and hide the blood in plain sight in several other bodies walking around, but then it would be like part of him lived on. I didn't want him to live on, which I know sounds absurd because his genetic material gave me two great kids. Still, I didn't think it fair to expose unsuspecting children and adults to whatever floated around in my ex's blood.

Disposing of twelve pints or less of blood would not be an easy task any other way. The best second option I had for disposing of that much blood unnoticed was to pour it into a river and let the large containers float down river in a storm such that the river and rainwater would wash away all traces. The containers would just be litter that someone threw in the river. No one would suspect much, and anyone who picked up trash along the banks would throw the containers away or recycle them.

There was something so satisfying about using my nursing skills to drain the life out of this son-of-a-bitch. It was more satisfying to realize that it would be fairly clean, and disposal of the evidence was relatively easy. For the first time in a long time, imagining the life-force drained from him and tossed away just as he had drained me and tossed me away brought me an overwhelming, albeit fleeting, sense of peace. I think I was getting closer and closer to a fully flushed out plan, even if exsanguination wasn't the route I finally chose.

Chapter 20: Death by Fear

After the divorce, my ex would go in spurts. There would be these really long, exceedingly quiet periods where occasionally I would wonder or worry if he was up to something. He almost always was, and that was the point. He loved playing mind games with anyone and everyone. It didn't matter if you were still in his life or not. He would find a way to make the proverbial other shoe drop just to mess with you.

Sadly, he would do this to the kids quite often as well. Frequently he would openly accuse me of manipulating them into hating him. I had chosen to ignore him except when the children were old enough and started asking me if something was seriously wrong with their father. I didn't outright tell them exactly what was wrong with their father. Instead, I'd ask them questions such as:

1. What makes you think there's something really wrong with your dad?
2. What have you experienced that you think isn't normal or right about your dad?
3. Why do you think that a behavior or example isn't normal?
4. What do YOU suppose is the problem with your dad?

The questions were suggested by therapists and experts who help kids that are traumatized by whacked out stuff a parent does to them. It helps children identify on their own what is wrong, why it isn't normal or healthy, and helps set them on a path to exploring what might be wrong with that parent mentally and emotionally. In this way, I wasn't flat-out badmouthing somebody that definitely deserved it. Rather, I was helping my children sort out what they were slowly starting to recognize as bizarre and psychologically toxic behavior.

As these things became more and more clear to my son, he began to watch and listen to his dad a little closer. One horrible night when the children were both supposed to be staying the weekend with their father, I got a call from our son. The boy was totally terrified. The sheer fear in his voice and the trembling I heard followed by choked back tears seriously worried me. My son could withstand just about anything his father had ever done, so what had happened to make him this scared?

As it turns out, he had witnessed his father knock his sister unconscious with a prescription medication that wasn't hers. The medication was his dad's. That is both illegal and dangerous, especially since she was only twelve. When she would come out of the unconscious state, her behavior would escalate to a violent and erratic state, a side effect of this particular medication when illegally used on children. No psychologist or psychiatrist would prescribe it for anyone under the age of 16 for this very reason.

I could hear the son-of-a-bitch screaming at our daughter in the background. I could hear our daughter throwing things and screaming back. Then I heard him threaten to incarcerate her or hospitalize her if she "didn't sit down and shut the f-ck up."

At one point, my son said he heard his dad slap his sister really hard. He said it sounded like a belt cracking before someone is whipped. I stopped short; how, HOW would my son know what a belt cracking sounds like unless he had experienced that firsthand?!?

I told my son to meet me outside in five minutes. I would try to get him away from there. He started crying hysterically as he thanked me. It was then that I knew that my son had reached his breaking point in fearing his father and he really didn't want to go back to staying with him if it could be helped.

Sadly, as I was picking my son up, their father came out, chasing after the boy and screaming furiously. It was definitely one of his hostile and awful moments in between periods of calm that I knew all too well. In the dark of night in the driveway it was an all-out screaming match. I tried to keep calm and not show emotion. I told the ex I needed Aidan's help to move things to storage where our daughter wasn't allowed to go. My ex "allowed" it on the condition I come straight back there and pick up our daughter because, as he put it, he "was done with her." A chill went down my spine. I know fear can kill you, if there is enough fear to create the adequate bodily response. I did not intend to die of fear that night or any night, nor would I let him continue to terrify the children.

As I went about my business, I thought about that fact. Fear is an autonomous response to stress. It causes the body to fight, flee, or become frozen to one spot, unable to act. My son had chosen to flee, and he had begged the one person he knew was safe to flee to. It momentarily made me warm and fuzzy inside knowing that this kid, both kids, felt safest with me. There would be no way my ex could ever undo the horrible damage he had done that pushed the children even closer to their mother.

I had chosen any one of the three responses in all the years I had been with him, eventually and finally choosing to flee for good. There is no shame in fleeing evil; it is the good and right thing to do. It's why it was so contradictory now for me to be thinking about doing something equally heinous to a monster of being. Returning to evil to do evil for the purpose of being free of that original evil seemed to cancel out the evil I intended to do. I started imagining what it would be like to make the bastard so utterly afraid that he would want to run and hide at the sight of me but be completely unable to move. Could I create enough fear in him to make him die?

People can and do die of fright all the time, especially those that suffer from anxiety and panic attacks, which my ex had regularly. The real question was in whether or not I could create the perfect storm of conditions that would cause him to go into panic attack and then into cardiac arrest as the end result. I really wanted to deliver the level of control and fear he had dealt me and the children through the years, to make him so afraid that he'd wet his pants and then just die. If I could make that happen, it would probably look like an accident. Given the anti-anxiety meds he had onboard, the coroner might even rule it an accidental death by panic attack. Given his history of consumption of high fat foods, sugary drinks, high cholesterol, fatty liver disease, and arteriosclerosis and atherosclerosis (narrowing and hardening of the arteries), it'd be a cinch to claim he died accidentally of fear, and I'd be off the hook.

So, what was he afraid of? I tried to remember what scared him the most, if anything. He wasn't afraid of spiders or rodents. He wasn't afraid of authority figures since he would just lie his ass off and charm them and then manipulate them into believing any story he wanted them to believe. He wasn't afraid of snakes either. He had zero fear of rollercoasters, which meant that creating a sense of heights and falling really fast wouldn't do anything. I did remember that he said something about a fear of doing any drug that involved a needle; he had tried everything but heroine because he knew heroine involved a needle and he didn't like that.

Given his psychological profile, I know he was both afraid of crowds and terrified of dying alone. It was a weird juxtaposition; don't go near crowds but don't die without someone beside you. I really couldn't do anything to recreate those particular anxieties to push him over the edge.

He never seemed to show some of the other typical anxieties that people have panic attacks about. I never saw him enter an elevator or cramped space and freak out. I never witnessed him losing it during a thunderstorm. Fire didn't seem to be bothersome either, which it would have been very strange if that were the case considering his two-pack a day cigarette habit.

Being without money did scare him. It scared him so bad he would do the most awful, hateful, selfish, nasty things to other people to get money from them. I suppose I could do something along those lines, such as tie him down and torture him until he gave up his banking information and then take whatever money he had and move it into an account he couldn't touch. I'd force him to watch the whole thing. Of course, that would never produce the level of anxiety I needed to arouse to cause a fatal heart attack.

A lot of pain and bleeding was not his thing either. I remember when I was in the throes of labor and he turned ashen gray and backed off into a corner of the room. The blood and pain of the delivery of the baby was intolerable to him; he couldn't stand it. He didn't leave the room, but he couldn't help the minute he saw an infant's head exiting my body. It was the one triumphant moment I had over him to see him look as though he might pass out. I remember that it happened with both deliveries of the children. Yes, a lot of bleeding and creating pain for him could cause the death by fear I was looking for.

Yet, how would I create that much blood and pain without his screams being noticed or his corpse obviously cut up in a very torturous sort of way? I didn't like anything messy that was traceable. The whole point to death by fear was that it wasn't messy and it looked accidental. Maybe I could bring up a basic conversation about what terrified each of the kids and then poke around at what scared the daylights out of him. God knows it wasn't horror flicks or slasher films or ghosts. All of those things were too tame for his twisted mind. Without knowing what really scared a monster, you can't scare the monster and kill it.

The idea of needles was intriguing. I shelved that idea and went back to thinking how intense the fear would have to be, where would I have to isolate him, time factors, and keeping his corpse in his own apartment versus moving it from my house or another location back to his apartment. That last part was not going to work at all and trying to execute by intense fear in his apartment would alert the neighbors to either side or downstairs.

I really wanted him to choke on his own fear. I wanted him to feel like every cell in his body was going to explode if he couldn't get away right at the moment fear was intensifying in him. But there was no real way to make this happen without several unknowns falling into place. It did make me feel the tiniest bit better imagining making him feel as terrified as our son had felt on the night the boy called out to me to come rescue him. The ex should feel that terrified in the final moment he took his last breath, and I did want to be there for that moment.

I just had to find exactly the right way or the right combination of approaches to make this plan fool-proof, or at least fool-proof enough for me to complete it and escape.

Chapter 21: Apparent Suicide

You can't change yourself if you don't want to change. You can't force someone else to change to be the person you really want either. I always knew that idiom of not changing someone if you really cared about him or her as a person, but it became quite clear to me after spending a few short years with my husband. He wasn't going to change. He didn't want to change. No amount of pressure I placed on him to accept therapy, get help, go to counseling as an individual or as a couple was going to happen.

Unfortunately, it took his attempt at suicide to make me really and fully understand that. *I* had a choice; stay with this person who I clearly did not love, trust, or feel safe with, or leave him. I could not be bound to the anchor that would drown me and kill me, so I chose to leave. What other adults in your life fail to tell you is that as long as you share children with an ex, you can never really leave. That anchor is always there. It is always weighing you down, pulling you under. You can kick, you can paddle, you can scream, and you can try to keep your head above the water line, but no divorce decree is ever really finite. That anchor you were so glad to be freed of is still there because you're expected to raise your children with it hanging around your neck.

I personally would never choose suicide. I wanted to run away. I wanted to flee. I wanted to put my children in a car and drive as far away as I could, but we live in an insane world where the law puts parents in jail for trying to start over and arrests parents when the other parents file charges for kidnapping.

So, I was stuck. I couldn't leave the state. I couldn't go anywhere and start a new life with my children. This monster who had tried to kill himself for attention and succeeded in getting attention but failing at ending his life was going to be around for many more years. His attempt at suicide was so utterly manufactured to look real that I often thought he had faked the whole thing to get back into the house with the children and I. Turns out, I wasn't far from the truth.

After seeing the basement rafters where he supposedly tried to hog-tie and hang himself, I knew. Even with as short as he was, he had faked the attempt because he could still touch the floor with one foot and undo the bonds he put on himself at any time. Who the *hell* fakes a suicide attempt to get what they want? Apparently, this guy does, because it got him exactly what he thought he wanted; to move back into the family home with a wife, toddler and newborn. He proceeded to sneer at how stupid everyone was for believing his trick and laughed at how "clever" he was in the attempt.

No one else would take him in after his "suicide" attempt. He had to be released and collected after spending only a week in a state mental hospital. He refused further treatment, and only visited therapists to downgrade the diagnosis he had been given. He made sure there was little else wrong with him besides "a little depression."

Part of me wished he had succeeded. Part of me really wanted him to have made a tiny mistake in how he attempted his fake suicide. I know people who really do want to die and who really have tried to kill themselves. I feel sorry for them because they are so devoid of hope and in so much need of help.

Not my ex. He reveled in what he had accomplished. He kept the cable from his attempted "suicide" around like it was a trophy. Hung it up in the corner of the back porch to "serve as a reminder" of what he did, what he could do, and what he could do again if he wanted to. That is some seriously twisted shit right there. He hung that cable right where I would see it, right where I would have to look at it going downstairs to dry laundry on an almost daily basis. Mind control, anyone?

Maybe what he needed was someone to show him what a really good and really believable attempt at suicide looks and feels like. There are a couple of different ways you can make a murder look like a suicide attempt, and because he had "attempted" it before, everyone would believe he had tried to kill himself a second time and succeeded. The cops would believe it too, if I did it just so.

Hanging by a rope, overdose on drugs, driving into a lake, accidental shooting while cleaning a gun, and swallowing a lot of pills were all of the usual ways in which people committed suicide or made a murder look like suicide. It was just a matter of picking a method and making sure none of my trace DNA was present. Rubber gloves with no powder in them were a must to keep fingerprints, handprints, and body oils from touching anything. A hair net or disposable surgical cap was necessary too. Anything involving a lot of blood meant I would have to cover myself in full surgical scrubs, but those could be burned or dumped in the trash can at work.

Creating a believable apparent suicide scene required planning every last detail and memorizing it perfectly in order such that nothing was left out and nothing was written down on paper or in a computer that would reveal murderous intent. I knew that rolling his car into a lake with the engine running and the windows down while he was unconscious would take monumental effort. It would have to be less complex and less public than that, although rolling his vehicle into a river or lake where he loved to fish would be quite believable.

Hanging himself again was also probable, forensically speaking. The vast majority of people who attempt suicide and survive often make a second attempt using the same or similar method as the first attempt. Rather than try something different, the idea is to "perfect" their chosen method of demise, and the statistics speak for themselves. However, there was no beam or hook or anything in his apartment that would have been high enough or strong enough to create this scene.

Accidental shooting suicide by gun was nearly impossible to get perfect because the angle of the gun meant sitting right behind him while trying to avoid shooting myself. Forensics could easily determine that the shot was not suicidal, and they may even determine it wasn't accidental. That was not a risk I was willing to take on any levels.

He's swallowed a lot of pills before that were not his own, and he's taken extra pills that were prescribed to him to get a desired effect. It would not be out of the realm of reality to force pills into him. It would only be impossible to get enough into him to kill him and make it look like a suicide.

A street drug overdose could work, but it needed a lot of finesse. Every step of such a plan would have to be in absolute order and absolutely perfect. As long as I was calm and collected and not rushed, it could work.

After so long and after so much research and deliberation, I turned my focus toward everything I had stashed in the back of my head. Every detail that I thought was feasible and therefore a possibility I began to pull together. As I did so, the years continued to blend one into the next. I could see the light at the end of the tunnel, and I wanted to charge it like a locomotive at top speed. I had to remind myself to pull back, just a little bit, for the kids' sake. I think I knew what I was going to do, and when I was going to do it. I just needed to start filling in the little blanks so that everything was methodical, and everything would blend together in just the most excellent way.

I should also have a backup plan and a backup step for each step of the plan. This was necessary in case one of the steps of the original plan went afoul and I had to turn to part or all of Plan B. I was really hoping that there would be no Plan B, but it became apparent that in order to control unforeseen variables and variants in the original plan, I had to know in an instant what I would do next. In essence, then, I had to create not one, but *two* perfect murder plans. My gut churned at the thought, but the plans would have to mesh and flow and interweave so perfectly that IF I needed to change course in a split second, I could.

It would take me much longer than I had originally hoped or expected to follow through. After all, the point was to have one flawless plan, but after a few years of thinking all of this through I realized that two flawless plans were necessary. I wasn't sure if my plan to rid the world of my ex would be adequate if it failed and I was unable to use some backup plan to make sure the desired intentions were well-executed.

There was also the memorization of both plans to help me remain calm under that kind of pressure. I wasn't totally insane; only someone with a penchant for killing others could be completely soulless, and I knew that wasn't me. I just had spent so much time with one person that was truly not worth the flesh in which he was encased that he had to go. Just one awful, evil, horrid excuse for a human that should not have been allowed to keep on living year after year and allowed to constantly torture those he claimed to care about. To keep myself steady and focused in a task I was not psychologically accustomed to doing regularly, I had to rely on an expert rote memory of what I was going to do and how I was going to do it.

101 Ways to Kill Your Ex, Part II:

What I Had to Learn Before Taking Action

As I spent all this time gathering ideas and imagining the perfect destruction for the "great destroyer of lives," a.k.a., my ex, I started picking up on things that would be vital to my efforts. I actually learned a lot about this process, including police forensics and how they figure out if something is a homicide, suicide, or accidental death. To be honest, good detective work relies heavily on technology these days, but it still takes a really sharp detective in charge of a case to figure things out and put the puzzle pieces together.

For me to kill my ex and have a few months to a few years of freedom, I had to "know thy enemy", or in this case, know the police adversaries that would probably be put in charge of any investigation into my ex's death. I would have to know how they think, what they would do, and what approaches they might use to uncover the truth. You can't bury your ex and bury the truth completely or indefinitely, but it is possible to escape from the hidden truth for a long time if you are careful, exact, clever, and mindful of every detail.

A police officer attempts to be mindful of every detail. They don't always get every detail, and they don't always get it right either. Details they think are important end up as "red herrings" or false clues, while important details that seem small, insignificant and therefore not details at all end up being really huge and particularly important. I had to figure out how a police officer would view the scene of my ex's untimely death, and then avoid the mistakes that would lead to my arrest.

Some police officers are quite smart. Others are not. I made a point of getting to know several of the local officers, especially when they entered the hospital with patients in need of emergency care or when prisoners were brought in that needed medical help. In my line of work, it wasn't difficult to make it seem as though some of the questions I asked were just general in nature and curious as to how they did their jobs and figured out this or that about the people they brought into the hospital.

I would ask things pertaining to domestic violence cases that seemed on track with the cases they brought in. Some of these questions hit closer to home for me than the police knew or would ever know or realize, but their answers provided me with a lot of information about how police work operates in a domestic violence case. Of course, these questions included:

1. If both parties are injured, how do you determine who's at fault for starting the episode?
2. Who do you arrest versus who do you take to the hospital?

3. Do you make an arrest first, and then help to the hospital, or do you provide medical help first and then arrest after the fact?

4. If nobody is physically injured, but both accuse the other of horrible behavior, is anyone arrested? How do you determine who to arrest when there is no sign of physical assault?

5. What happens when someone files a false report of domestic violence and there's no substantial or corroborating evidence to prove otherwise? In other words, if a person calls the police for help with a domestic disturbance and the other person involved says nothing happened but the caller insists something did, how do you determine who's telling the truth?

6. What happens if someone has a mental health issue that you don't know about, and he or she is the one accusing the other person of bad behavior? Do you feel bad for arresting the wrong person or for taking that person into custody when it is the mentally unstable partner that is filing the false report?

7. Have you ever met a sociopath and absolutely knew he or she was a sociopath? What about psychopaths?

Of course, some of these questions I just brought up into conversation naturally so as to keep things light and not make the cops suspicious. If they gave me some "side eye" I would simply laugh it off and tell them I was curious about how they would know or decide to handle situations like these when something seemed off or not right. They would laugh then and tell me what I wanted to know. It's how I got to know their lines of thinking, and how I got to know most of the officers that would probably be on duty when I carried out my plan.

Another thing I learned was that the best alibi is the most ridiculously obvious one. If no one can place you at the crime scene, great, but something as simple as a single strand of hair could screw up the most flawless plan for murder. Hugging the kids before they visited their dad and allowing my naturally shedding hair to collect on their clothes and transfer to their dad's apartment was one way to do this.

Another way was to actually engage police officers in conversations about murder, accidental deaths and suicides outside of office hours. I quickly learned that a really good "alibi" was to invite officers to a coffee break while I was at work or ask them if I could buy them lunch and then discuss things I wanted to know. I would tell them I was working on a book that would be a murder mystery, or something that would discuss statistics on these particular cases in our fair city. Since cops often like to talk about work without revealing too many details, they took the bait. It would be very hard later to come back and accuse me of anything by pointing out these lunches or coffee breaks where we talked about their profession in a general way when I could just as easily point these things out as "research for my book."

Better still, I could write whatever book I was pretending to write. Keeping detailed notes of our conversations and then integrating the information on a story on my computer at home acted as a strange sort of alibi, but it would only prove what I had been telling the police all along. I was collecting information from them to write a book, not to kill my ex-husband. It creates reasonable doubt in the minds of a jury, should I ever be caught and tried. Writing a book about death and police investigative tactics is not evidence of an actual murder planned and executed. At least, it never has been, and it could prove to be a most useful tactic in my plan.

Another approach was to get to know the police on a more personal level. My kids actually helped with this, even though they didn't' realize it at the time that they were creating situations that would lead to the perfect murder of their father. I pause here for a moment to think about that, as it is a very strange sentence. It makes my stomach flip-flop, as if I had involved my kids in the plot intentionally. In truth, these encounters with the police and my children were really random; I didn't plan any of it, and I tired to avoid them. However, lacking any help from their father meant that sometimes I needed help from a crisis hotline, and the police officers were the ones that would respond.

Ergo, I became friendly with many officers. I recognized who they were by name, personal details, and how they each thought about things. They learned a lot about me and my children in return. We were almost friends with most of the police force, which is important because you should always keep friends close and enemies closer. I kept the police officers as close as I dared, leading them to believe I was a good and decent person, a wonderful mother to challenging children, and someone in need of their help. When people think nothing but positive things about you, their personal perception of you is skewed such that they cannot begin to consider you for anything heinous, and I knew this all too well. I could thank the ex for teaching me that, since it was he who had used such tactics in the past. I was now using some of those tactics in a way that would turn the tables on him for good.

Another thing I learned was that people are always suspicious of anyone that keeps to themselves. Usually, people that avoid contact with others do so for two reasons. One, they have a lot of ugly stuff to hide, or two, they are desperate to remain private in their daily lives. I had always lived the latter, but now I realized that continuing to live quietly in solitude made me suspect for what I hoped to achieve. I had to slowly and carefully make myself a more public figure, initiating contact with neighbors, talking to people in the neighborhood, appearing very friendly and going so far as to invite people over for lunch or coffee just to visit. It meant a lot more work with keeping house and keeping children in line, but I had to make it seem like I wasn't the type to randomly kill people either. I had to be the type of person no one suspects of murder or would ever consider a dangerous person.

I also went out of my way to be a model nurse. Always there, always working hard at work and picking up shifts for others to take vacation and always bringing in food or treats for the rest of the staff. I gained a ton of acceptance points with others at work, and I made a concerted effort to be nice to those I really didn't like at work. It was almost more stress than I could bear, but it was vital to my plan. There could not be a single person alive that could point to me and say, "She's dangerous and she killed her ex." Every last person I encountered had to love me and be in utter disbelief that I could harm anyone.

In truth, I really couldn't harm most people. I was a nurse, after all, and I did enjoy helping people and occasionally saving a life. At least that much was believable for others around me, which did make things a little easier with all the pretend niceties I had to endure. It doesn't mean I liked all people, nor that I really liked people in general. That seems weird to a lot of people who assume that nurses really love working with people, but you have to understand that in order to do this job a long time, you often have to emotionally distance yourself from every patient. It's a weird little dance where you care somewhat, pretend to care a lot, but may actually not really care at all because of the emotional and psychological toll it takes on you. All of that combined with the fact that I was married and then divorced from someone who forced me into emotional and psychological survival mode for years meant that I had to pretend to care most days out of the year just to get through the requirements of the job.

So, it was a constant game of appearances and pretend. I was careful not to reveal much about my personal life or self. I was careful not to say too much about my marriage and divorce. In fact, I decided at one point to quietly hide most details of my marriage and divorce and not allow them to enter the conversation beyond anything related to the kids and their court-ordered time with the ex. Busybodies abound, and you never know which person will betray you if you provide them with too much information.

Different aspects of crime scene investigation came next. I had to learn about fingerprinting and how it was done. I had to learn how you could tell if fingerprints were faked or real, and whether or not they were imprinted on something in a very natural sort of way. A misplaced fingerprint on any object meant that it could throw an entire investigation off the course I wanted it to go, making my imminent capture or arrest closer than I wanted it.

So, I did what any sane person would do; I ordered a fingerprinting kit and checked out books on fingerprinting. I had the kids make copies of their fingerprints and then I made a game of it. They had to touch things in the house they weren't allowed to touch, and then I had to figure out just by fingerprinting and matching fingerprints who the culprit was. In essence the kids became the perfect teachers for learning how people touch things, pick things up with their fingers and hands, and how vastly different fingerprints are for each individual. Additionally, anyone wanting to know why I was so keen on fingerprinting would receive the overprotective parent answer of protecting the kids in the event that the kids were kidnapped and left a fingerprint trail for me to follow. It seemed like a perfect logical reason for learning fingerprinting and turning it into a game for the children.

Learning fingerprinting helped me learn about handed-ness too. The way left-handed people held objects was very different from the way right-handed people held objects. Neither of my children were left-handed, so I made that a game too. I would tell them to use their nondominant hand to try to trick me into thinking it wasn't them so I could see how they might pick up objects with their left hands. It was a highly effective teaching tool. I also had a good friend who was left-handed, and she had a lot of fun sharing with me how she picked things up with her left hand. Perhaps most interesting of all was learning that left handedness was associated with sinister and evil people. That particular old wives' tale certainly suited my ex, who was left-handed. As far as I was concerned, there was no other more sinister or more evil than he.

I recalled such an evil moment when our children were sound asleep in the back seat of the car. We had been returning from a trip to a huge zoo where the children had been run ragged until they were too tired and too crabby to do anything else. It was a sad year for the children and I as it was the same summer where this twisted bastard was putting on a good show by playing daddy dearest.

On the ride home, while the children were asleep, I tried to appeal to any softness in him as a parent. I begged and pleaded for him to give the children back to me. I argued that they were too small to be without their mother. I tried so hard to get him to give me a reason why he would not let the children just come home instead of putting them through the trauma and the hell of being separated from me for so long. I steered clear of his deranged idea that I was an unfit mother; I knew I wasn't.

He refused to tell me why he wouldn't stop this horrible mess he was creating with courts and social workers and false accusations. He grinned, enjoying the pain and torture that was obvious on my face. He finally pretended to cave to give me an answer, and I knew the answer would be the ugliest thing he could say to me to make me cry because that's exactly what he wanted and what he was looking for.

"You can't have the children back because you *suck at being a parent*!" He sneered with such a malicious smile. Of course, I cried. He wanted me to cry. I figured if I gave him exactly the emotion and the response he was looking for, he'd acquiesce. He didn't.

That was just a small bit of what he wanted to do to me, and by extension, to them. The sick thing is that he didn't see his actions as harming them at all. In his deranged mind he believed to some extent that he was *saving* them. He couldn't see the pain in their little faces and the desperation in their cries to go home to their mom, the one person who had always been there for them and would never intentionally or willingly leave them with their father.

I think he knew I would never leave them with him. He wanted a battle royale, one where he would come out on top, and the children would see their father as a hero. He had left us so many times and left the children without a father or someone who cared enough to stick around. This new act, this new show he was putting on for the courts, the police, and the social workers was more about punishing me and making me as miserable as he could. He did punish me, but it didn't last. His own failings and failures as a human being caught up to him, and both children ended up back with me for a very long time. However, the damage he did lasted even longer.

Snapping out of this distant and awful memory, I continued to work on learning everything about fingerprints. When I was satisfied with the knowledge and experience I needed to make sure my fingerprints would never appear at the crime scene, I moved on to another topic that I would need to know; trace evidence. This I made into a game with the children too.

Trace evidence is literally anything you leave behind that can be discovered by a microscope during an investigation of the body, an autopsy, and/or a thorough sweep of the crime scene. This could be skin cells, hairs from my head, chemicals left on lips or teeth, powder from a powdered surgical glove, bits of fiber from a rope or twine, etc. To carry out the perfect murder, I had to know every detail the police would look for, and then make sure that I could easily erase those details from the crime scene, prevent such details, or have a plausible reason for some details to be present (e.g., a hair from my head in his apartment when I was not allowed to enter for years).

It could also be random strings from an article of clothing, a cat or dog hair, a bit of dirt not found near his apartment but evident near my home. It could be anything that is even slightly out of place that could not be explained away with an answer that made sense. A lot of people who try to plan the perfect murder think that shaving all the hair off of one's body, avoiding any lotions, perfumes, ointments, or creams, and thoroughly exfoliating the body hours before killing someone will eliminate the trace evidence a murderer leaves behind. Sadly, it doesn't. It's a step in the right direction to reduce the possibility of leaving something of yourself behind, but it's not foolproof. I also wasn't about to completely shave and wax my entire body and head within days of his intended demise, so I would have to be particularly careful about trace evidence.

In this case, I had the children leave little clues around the house. A string from some unknown item, like a towel or scarf, left on a pillow or closed in a door helped me learn just how careful to be. I called the game "playing detective", and they loved it. When they got haircuts, we'd keep a few hairs and leave them around the house for me to find. I would have to look under a microscope at the hair to tell whose it was. They liked looking at stuff under the microscope too, so it was fun for them. Traces of dirt from their shoes, small stones or pebbles, and even grasses, weeds, and bits of flowers helped me find where my children had been and how to avoid going to those places to avoid collecting that kind of trace evidence on myself. This kind of thing can attach to you and drop off anywhere in someone else's home, which leads to the discovery by police that someone that doesn't live there has been there.

Literally anything I could possibly think of as something that could turn up in my ex's apartment and create problems for me later became part of the "playing detective" game. It eventually became a challenge to see which child could come up with something I couldn't decipher. I was building stronger and stronger bonds with them every day, teaching them invaluable skills about the world around them, and silently and quietly teaching myself all I would need to know to avoid capture and arrest in the future.

Maybe part of the reason why I finally included them in what I was doing was to persuade them that their mother wasn't evil. I wanted them to know, when all was said and done, that I loved them, and I did what I did to free us all. I didn't think they would believe that unless they could see for themselves that either their father was truly awful, or that I had done everything I could for years to protect them from the worst of his unconscionable behavior. I couldn't make them see how twisted their father was, and I knew that even attempting to do so would make them turn against me. Instead, I focused on making our bonds unbreakable. If nothing could break the strength of our mutual love and affection between children and mother, they would never believe that their mother had killed their father. At the very least, they might never accept that their mother was guilty, and I'd be happy enough with that.

Having them help me learn the many things that would keep me from getting caught helped draw us closer together. They were learning science, medicine, math, and more. They would never know they were an integral part of their mother's plan to murder their father. I was so certain of the strength of our bonds now that I felt safe and carefree in my decision to move forward with my plans. There was still a little more to learn to keep me safe, and it would require more time than I had intended for the ultimate plan (with the backup plan!), but this time with my children was as precious to me as the end result of my chosen plan.

The next thing I needed to know about was rope. We spent hours looking at rope, testing it for tensile strength, and discovering if it left any fibers behind if somebody twisted against it or it was tied too tight. When I was younger, we would play "Cowboys and Indians" in the yard. Then, it wasn't insulting or taboo to tie up the "cowboys" or tie up the "Indians". It was just something kids played. I created a variation of it that would allow the children and I to see if we could escape the bonds and find traces of different kinds of rope on our clothes or skin. Not only did this teach me a lot about all different kinds of rope, twine, yarn, and cable, but it taught my children how to escape bonds in the event that they were ever kidnapped and tied to something. Because it was all in good fun (or so they thought), no one ever came to harm or felt scared. It was valuable information for me, and priceless survival skills for them.

We even learned about all kinds of knots you could tie with rope. So, so many knots used to secure boats, parts of boats, horses and cattle, and even tents and rigging for temporary shelters were explored. This game helped us determine what knots were very secure and what knots could easily be slipped and untied in a hurry. I think that was a very valuable skill for all of us, since knot tying could be used in almost every aspect of daily life no matter where you were or what you were doing. For me, it had its obvious uses later on.

I learned some knots I could use to keep someone tied up just long enough to follow through on a simple task without leaving any marks on the skin. Slip knots could be tight or loose, but the thing or being secured by a slip knot could slip the bonds if enough wriggling, tugging or pulling occurred. Ergo, what I needed was knots that were more secure without leaving marks or trace evidence. Once I figured out what those were, I practiced them often on the kids and on myself, allowing the kids to tie me with these knots to a chair to play a game I called "escape like a magician". It worked like a charm.

Next, I realized that sedating someone quickly was necessary. Recalling that just about any plan for killing someone would require subduing the target quickly and quietly, I had to understand my options. The kids were not part of this of course, since I would never involve them with any drugs or dangerous chemicals. Instead, I had to use lab mice as my unwilling research victims. I kept several mice in cages in my lab in the basement. I told the kids I was working on something important and that they could play with the mice when I was done with my research if they stayed out of my lab. That seemed to quell their curiosity sufficiently. The lock on the lab door was a definite deterrent as well.

For another few months I worked with some of the widely used anesthesia medications commonly found in a hospital. I even tested some of the older ones, like ether and halothane. These were a little harder to come by, but they might be enough to throw an investigation off course as no one my age would remember or know enough about them to use them for the purpose I intended. I eventually scrapped that notion based on the fact that the most "original" of ideas often lead to the most evidence against you.

In a murder, the most common of things is the most difficult of police investigations to solve and resolve because the items involved can be bought or acquired anywhere. It's the biggest reason why serial killers get caught; their "signature" method or approach gives them away. In their attempt to be unique or different from other historical killers, they end up supplying the police with exactly the right clues to catch and imprison them, a mistake I had no intention of making.

Chloroform was a little "old school", but it was also the most widely sold and easily acquired of the general anesthetics. A few drops on a rag were all that was needed to sedate a wriggling, fighting, breathing adult. However, it took too long for sedation to kick in; five minutes was the minimum amount of time. There was no way I could hold him that long.

I could inject him with Ketamine, known on the street as "special K". It was possible for me to sneak up behind him and inject him with a dose. I would have to wrestle with him for about a minute or two, unless I made the dose a little bigger than is standard. It would take some careful calculations to get it right without killing him. However, the drug would be in his system, and it could not have any counterproductive interactions with anything else I might inject into him.

If I had something like ether or chloroform to use, I had to choose a very common rag for this purpose too, or risk blowing my plan all to pieces. I thought about using standard wound gauze you can find in any over-the-shelf first aid kit, but the fibers of this product could leave behind bits if my target bit the gauze or microscopic fibers went up his nose. I had to find something that would not unravel or leave a trace of textile dust. That was more difficult and time consuming than choosing a method of quick acting sedation.

It was also necessary to ensure that any chloroform would not remain on his skin. Once inside his nose and traveling through his bloodstream, it would disseminate over a few minutes and the effects would wear off quickly, but I didn't want traces of the chloroform on his skin under his nose or on his lips after the fact. I found the right agent to remove traces of liquid-to-gas from skin and made sure I had the perfect amount stashed in an applicator bottle with soft tip for later.

Assembling a "murder kit" or a "torture kit" was dangerous. If caught, the police would know exactly what they were looking at. I had to keep components of what I needed in places where it made sense to find such things and not all together where they would look out of place or suspicious. Reasonable doubt can be created if nothing used to eliminate someone is found next to something else in your house. For example, you wouldn't put the sedation next to the rope and rubber gloves. Instead, put the rubber gloves in the first aid kit, the rope in the garage, and the sedation agent with solvents and cleaning supplies. Better yet, get rid of some of the items after use, or make the items as ordinary as possible to follow through on an appearance of innocence.

Timing is everything in these situations. While an alibi is priceless, I knew there was no real way to create an alibi that wouldn't later be discovered or ruled out. Even the use of delayed text messages to someone from my phone while I left my phone at home could be untangled by a good IT detective. As smart as that idea might be, IT people are faster and smarter than that, and police stations are hiring such skilled intellects to figure out things like delayed messaging faster than perpetrators of crimes can figure out how to use such tricks.

Ergo, I had to find the perfect window of time. This window of time would only allow me to get in, get the job done, get out, and get out of the country as fast as I could all without drawing attention. It had to seem like something the bastard would do to himself but still let me off the hook. As long as I had children to raise, I didn't think it possible. I might have to abandon them, even if the perfect window of opportunity opened itself to me. I wasn't sure I could do that, much less manage the inevitable aftermath of leaving them behind.

Back to the drawing board I returned again and again. The biggest prevention of knocking off my ex were the children. They were so important to me, but I didn't want them to be the sole reason for me to veer off course in this grand scheme of mine. The inner turmoil was fractious. I now understood how those who killed often and seemed to kill without feeling had to have been emotionless toward their victims because it felt nearly impossible for me to do this heinous thing without worrying about the two people in the world I cared most about.

If it weren't for the children, I probably could have done this a long time ago, but I might have also done it in haste. The old adage of "haste makes waste" applied here. A hastily planned murder is one that makes waste of both the victim and the killer, and it is left with imperfections in its execution. There could be no imperfections or flaws here. There could be no distractions or poor timing.

I reflected on the fact that if I had divorced him without children involved, or if we had never married (which, quite honestly, would have been the best choice I had ever made), his life might not end at my hands. Then I thought about all the horrible, awful things he did, all the selfish, asinine things he did, and all the moronic, stupid things he did, and I was sure that if I weren't the one ending his life, someone else would have. There is also the distinct probability that he would have ended his own life at some point, given his major mental health conditions. Perhaps the reason I could still consider doing this was that it was less of a mercy killing for the rest of us and more of a mercy killing for him, except that taking that stance on the matter made my stomach churn and pre-vomit acid rise in my throat.

That was the same sensation, the same skin crawling, acid rising, pre-vomit feeling I got every time I saw him and every time someone said his name out loud. They wanted me to say his name, but I couldn't. If I tried, I felt like vomiting and I had to contain myself to keep from trembling. The world out there, my family, and even most of my friends did not know half the horrors he had done. I had vowed never to tell them so that they would not guess that he had died at my hand. But his name, his putrid awful name, was something I could never say ever again. I always distanced myself from him in every way I could and spoke in generalities when I spoke of him. It was the only way I could maintain some semblance of control over the reactions my body had to his name and his psychological, emotional, and physical proximity to me.

I came back from the brink. I came back and crawled out of a pit. I came back from many moments of awful memories and bad moments. I was almost free. His death would finally free me completely, and that was exactly what I wanted. I wanted that freedom; that sense that he could not have any sort of hold on me anymore.

Time stands still and is surreal when you're a victim of an abuser. You are always outside yourself looking down, looking in, and imagining that you must have crossed over into the twilight zone. I remember feeling exactly that way on the morning of my wedding. It felt so surreal. I couldn't believe it, and it took me days after the marriage to come to grips with being connected to this "other". By then, it was too late for me to unsee and not experience so much in a few short weeks. I realized I had to escape then, and escape was exactly the word I meant. Timing was everything. Timing was everything then, and timing was everything now.

It has to look like I was leaving the country for good. It has to look like I wasn't going to run away from something criminal, but instead heading towards a future I had planned a long time. It had to be safe for the children, too. It had to look like they had no knowledge or part in it, even though I had in some ways involved them already. It had to be the perfect moment, the perfect opportunity, and I had to wait for it, plan for it, watch for it, and then quietly pounce before disappearing.

I used to think that killing him was awful but easy. Killing someone isn't easy at all. A hundred years ago it might have been easy, but the times in which we live have made it nearly impossible. So many advances in science and forensics make it easy for police to catch up to killers. Even serial killers can't avoid capture forever. I honestly couldn't fathom how anyone could kill on a regular basis, kill without much feeling, kill without fear or remorse, and kill without trepidation. Of course, this would be my first, last, and only killing. Maybe that was the actual hesitation in the problem. I wasn't going to "practice kill" either, which meant that this was going to be the hardest thing I've ever done or would ever do.

The last and final thing I had to teach myself was psychology of the human mind. It wasn't just about how he thought; I certainly had experienced enough of his thinking firsthand. It had to be about what I thought, what I intended to do and why I intended to do it. This was vital because I had to make it all look like something I'd never do, never intend to do, and make it look quite the opposite of the mind that would be bereft of human anger and revenge. Half of any police investigation is psychological. They want to know why you did it and what motivated you to do it.

When you know what direction your pursuers will take in attempting to find the person responsible, you can rethink your steps to see if there is some way you can lead them astray and send them on wild goose chases. The problem with most killers is that they aren't that smart. They don't spend years planning to kill, and they don't educate themselves about how police and police investigations operate. Most killers who think they are smart are actually quite dumb, and that is what trips them up.

Thinking you are really smart and very clever and that you will elude the police is a major mistake. It's arrogance that causes killers to think that how they do something will trick the cops and that the killers will get away with their crimes. I was careful never to assume that I was extremely clever or overly intelligent. I knew that I was very smart, but I worked hard at keeping humble so that my own arrogance would not be my undoing.

I read a lot on books on serial killers, watched shows that interviewed police who worked serial killer cases, and got to know and study the minds of the officers involved in those cases. Were the officers themselves arrogant? If an officer is arrogant, it's likely he or she will make some serious mistakes during the course of their investigations or careers as well. It is the nature of being proud and boastful; you lose sight of things to which you should pay attention.

I wasn't worried about my interest in serial killers. A lot of people have bizarre hobbies. There are even some people that like to visit murder scenes of former serial killers because they are so into the subject. I wasn't into the subject, but I could certainly pretend I was if I thought it would help me narrowly miss arrest. If anyone wanted to point to my reading materials or videos at this time, I had reasons lined up for miles.

The point was to dig deep into the psychological aspects. There was adequate reading material and viewing material on the subject, including journals of psychological investigative papers and true crime shows. I really tried to get to the meat of these minds, both the minds of the criminals and the minds of those who investigated the crimes. It's a game of chess between hunter and hunted. If you know the players and pieces really well, you can always remain ten steps ahead of what is happening.

I had some experience in this already. Having been married to a mind that was constantly spinning, constantly scheming, constantly trying to throw shade on anyone else but himself, I had learned to stay well ahead of what he did. Perhaps the best practice I had in this was when I fired my lawyer and went to work on a new court case as my own defender.

He had left our son with us, supposedly for just a short time. He told the poor boy he was just going to live somewhere else for a couple of months until he could get a new apartment. I knew he was lying through his teeth because my ex's landlord had called me looking for him. My ex had abandoned the apartment and left some things behind while taking the bare minimum in other things. That was how he operated.

Almost a year went by, and I was forced to continue perpetuating this lie to my son that his father was going to come back and they were going to live together again. The children had to visit their father in the basement of their grandmother's home, and they were not allowed upstairs to play or use the restroom while they were there. My ex didn't pay rent to his mother, and she didn't want any more kids around if she could help it.

My heart was breaking when I would drop them off and know they would be in a basement full of damp, bugs, spiders and other creepy crawly things that would make their way over my children at night. That's no way to live, but it's not as though their father cared. He insisted on his parental right to see the children, and this is how it was done at the time. I finally gave him an ultimatum; find suitable housing or give the custody and placement back to me fully. He ignored me completely.

My lawyer had not been much help before, so I started to write down everything I knew my ex would lie about and come after me for. I made sure that every which way he could twist something in court, I had a response for it. It was an exercise in knowing exactly how to counter every move he might try to make. I dug up pages and pages of factual information on the internet, got professionals to back me with documentation of their own, and provided financial records up to one decade old to show who was actually the financially responsible one and who wasn't. I dug deep into the ugly annals of our history together to find what I needed, and prayed it was enough.

When court dates arrived, my ex had secured proper housing literally three days before the hearing. He could have done it much sooner, but he didn't. He waited until it was useful for him to do so. He tried to avoid parental responsibilities, tried to take the house from me on a technicality, and he was bent and intent on making me homeless so he could secure full custody of the children. There's no better way to do that than to try to force your ex-spouse into a homeless situation, despite the fact that you're not interested in the house whatsoever.

Thankfully, I had learned a lot from the psychological warfare I had been through with him. I learned all the right things to say in court, all the right things to do, all the right evidence to gather and all the right professionals to circle my proverbial wagon. Blessings abounded, and there was nothing he could really do when the children were allowed to live with me more and restricted from living with him going forward. That's all I really wanted too, to know that the kids would have the least amount of contact possible, and that they would have almost equal contact because he refused to have contact with our daughter at all. Later, parts of me wished I could have undone some of that request, because our daughter suffered so much at the hands of her father that I realized no contact with a father like that is better than forced contact on a brief basis.

It was check and checkmate from that point on. I was concerned that somehow any future financial successes or inheritances I might achieve or receive would be pursued by him. He was a greedy, selfish pig after all. I figured he might try to pursue my financial gains in the future by claiming I should have paid child support in spite of the fact that it was I who had been with the kids most often and I who had never left them to pursue my own selfish desires and perceived "needs." Courts could not create any statute that would prevent him from doing this to me, so I knew that I would have to be on guard as the years passed by.

Of course, now that I had my plan in place and I was almost ready, future financial gains and losses were irrelevant. He couldn't touch anything of mine at any time. My children, my home, my possessions, my money, my hopes and my dreams would all be rid of him. I had studied, read, tested, and learned everything I needed to know, and then some, to bring the plan to fruition and still escape for years to come.

The Light at the End of a Very Long and Very Dark Tunnel

Twenty years of my life stolen. Twenty years waiting in agony and constantly being tortured by this beast who just would not go away. Sometimes I think about time machines, and what would happen if I could go back in time and just stop everything from happening. Where would I be? I'm sure I'd be happier, at least that's what I like to think and what I tell myself. I spent all this time thinking, plotting, waiting, planning.

You see, the biggest problem with acting on your revenge plan is that you act in haste. In situations where divorce exists and there have been some pretty ugly situations between you and your ex, the police always question you first. You are their first target. But if you wait, if you hold it down, no matter how insane you feel and how much you want to react *now*, it's better. You can point at the fact that if you were guilty, your ex-husband would have been dead a long time ago. You can point out that you have been divorced and have been tortured by this ass for this long and you did nothing, so why would you kill him now?

It makes more sense, doesn't it? Who would question that? What member of any jury would look at the long and abusive history I've had with this jerk and think to themselves, *"Yeah, she did it. After all these years, she did it."* I don't think most of them could ignore the history of non-violence and really believe that I suddenly decided to finally kill the bastard, and that's the perfect way to do it. The waiting and suffering in silence nearly killed me, but I knew it would finally be worth it. It also gave me plenty of time to think, and to plan.

First, there was the issue of the kids. Oh, how I languished over this! Seriously, the end results of seeking revenge sooner were not good for anyone. In fact, I could predict umpteen nightmares for them, and it was worse than anything I could ever dream up for their father.

If I had killed him when the kids were barely teenagers, they could have ended up in the system. Sexually abused, raped, beaten, and in the system is a horrifying reality. Becoming runaways and prostitutes was another. However, I think the image that horrified me most was his asinine family fighting for custody of one or both of the kids, and not because they really cared, but because they were greedy, selfish, lazy bastards like him.

Oh, my Lord in Heaven above! *There* was a whole mess of corrupt and stupid! I could just see my daughter pregnant at sixteen because his family runs around the minute, they figure out what genitals are for. My son would be in jail before he hit eighteen, and the bastards would be robbing my kids blind of their disability money. It made me utterly sick.

I wanted to cry, because I knew no one in my family would ever take both kids, if they took either of them at all. My daughter might go with my mother but given the way my mother tried to turn me into her little "mini-me," and that she was EXACTLY like my ex, I just couldn't. Then my son would still be in the system, because nobody wanted to take on the challenges of an autistic teenager with a temper. I had to wait, even when I was desperate and couldn't take it anymore, I had to wait—for their sakes.

Which is how all the research panned out for me, and the waiting did too. The ex spent the last few years living above yet another drug dealer. The stupid ass denied it, but all the signs were there. People on welfare don't raise pit bulls in the backyard, drive luxury vehicles, and have strange characters coming and going at all odd hours. Nope, drug dealers. My kids spent time with their father above a drug dealer's abode, and jackass played it off as stupid. No court would listen to that either without proof.

Then there was the park just down the block. The park was in the news regularly because of people finding used heroin needles in the grass while walking their dogs. Duh. It doesn't take much to make this connection, does it? Nope, but King Stupid denied that, saying I was full of shit, saying it didn't happen, it was not real. I was just grateful my kids never went down to that park and got stuck with one of those non-existent needles in the grass. Idiot.

Of course, all of this circumstantial stuff really made it that much easier for me. Sure, I had never bought drugs in my life, but I could make it work. Not like the drug dealers downstairs would ever tell. I just had to intercept one of their customers to confirm and make sure I could get what I was looking for.

Timing was really everything. It had to be after my daughter finished high school. She was my youngest, and I wanted to make sure she didn't screw up her life before graduation. That's all you really have to do anyway, see them to their eighteenth birthdays and make sure they graduate high school so that they are not complete losers like the ones you married and divorced. What the kids choose to do with their lives after that is their own business.

My daughter turned eighteen eight months before she graduated. That was a long and agonizing eight months, to be sure. However, it did give me an excellent exit strategy.

I announced that as soon as she was done with high school, we'd take a little trip to France. I've always wanted to go there, live there, become an ex-pat. There is SO much about France that is better than the U.S., bar none. France got social reform right when the U.S. got it totally wrong. That is where I wanted to be my whole life.

I began filing for an ex-patriot exit to France early in the school year. I was leaving, and fully intent on never coming back. The kids were just taking a trip with me, as far as anyone else knew. They were free to return to their native country at the end of the tour if they wanted to, and I had already planned to encourage them to go back or move on. Their choice, their lives.

I didn't even tell my family. Sure, I had been talking about living in the south of France for years, but that fit neatly into my plan too. If the police ever came looking for me, they would look there first, but probably not find me. I have one of those faces and bodies that looks very different and can be changed easily to look like a completely different person. I knew that from the time I first got glasses as a kid. Glasses on, different looking person. Glasses off, totally different looking person. Twenty-five pounds lost or gained, and I could blend into a crowd. Dye my hair any color, and you could never find me. In France, I could do all the above and evade the police and extradition for years. Cornered, I could walk into a church and ask for asylum, and no one could touch me. I had this part covered.

As for living expenses, well, ex-pats could get 500 Euros just for denouncing their American citizenship and living in France. That wasn't much, but I had spent decades of my life living hand-to-mouth. This was no different. If I scrimped, I could do it.

Finally, the day came. The kids had their passports, which no longer needed the bastard's signature because they were now officially adults. He would never have allowed them to leave the country before. He would never have signed off on their passports when they were underage. More control, of course. That's okay, it was almost over.

The kids were packing and signing off to friends over social media. Our ride to the airport was only a few hours away. I had spent the last couple of years pretending to be the nicest, sweetest ex-wife I could ever be. Lower his suspicions—that was the plan. Quietly, stealthily, waiting to pounce.

I made a call to the jerk. Told him I needed something of the kids from his place. Went up the back stairs to his only exit door. Like the unsuspecting fool he had become, he let me in.

My gut was swirling and spinning, but I was ready. As soon as he turned his back, I pulled my gloved hands out of my pockets with the rag I had already chloroformed minutes before. His fat, bloated body wriggled in the crook of my arm as I struggled to control him and keep the rag over his mouth and nose. He almost got loose. He tried to yell, but I got control of the situation. All that weight training with my son through his teen years also paid off in that very moment.

Once I was absolutely sure he was out, I set the scene in the kitchen. I dragged his fat, old punk ass into the kitchen, keeping the chloroformed rag on his face. Man, he was a heavy bastard! I pulled him into the chair I had pulled out from the table.

Next, I tied him up. In case he was faking, I didn't want him to move. I made sure to use a rope product that didn't leave trace fibers. No fibers means that no police can prove this wasn't what I wanted it to look like. Still gloved, I pulled out the fresh needle, the bent spoon, and the tiny ball of heroin in a bag. It didn't look like much, but the dealer downstairs said to portion carefully because it was enough to kill you. That's all I needed to hear at the time.

His veins had always been huge. You could see them right through his skin. It was the biggest reason why he could spend years donating his toxic plasma for money. It made me sick to think of all the people who needed plasma and would be getting his psychotropic medications along for the ride. Yet, it did make this so much easier. The track marks on his arms would probably be perceived as his regular use of the drug.

I used the spoon to scoop the heroin out of the bag. I never touched it, not once, to avoid any residue on my gloves. I suppose it didn't really matter; my exam gloves would never be found anyway, and since they did not have powder in them, no one would know the gloves were ever there. But I also did not want any of that poison in my system, because that would be a tip-off if I was caught before this all worked my way.

I held the lighter under the spoon. It took longer than I thought, and I started to get a little nervous. Finally, the heroin was liquid. Carefully, I took the needle and drew up every last drop. I almost giggled thinking about how I had started this journey thinking about poisons and how women resort to them, but then focused on the task at hand.

Releasing his right arm (because he was left-handed), I tied the rubber hose around the arm just above the elbow. Years working as a nurse played into this moment too, and I suddenly realized just how much of my life had built to this very moment and this very act. It was surreal.

Tapping his arm, I got a vein to pop right away. Pushing the needle into and across the vein, I carefully drew back the plunger. A little blood—good, the needle was right where it needed to be. I shoved the plunger all the way down and left the needle in his arm.

Of course, now I had to be sure that everything had his fingerprints on it. Staging a suicide by accidental overdose on heroin is quite a feat. A clean hose and a clean needle would be dead giveaways. I opened his mouth and stretched the end of the hose closest to his mouth toward his gaping maw. Then I forced his mouth shut, as though he would have used his teeth to bite one end of the hose to draw it tight around his arm, then let it go. Next, he had to touch the needle, the bag, the spoon and the lighter.

I had spent years thinking about how someone in this position would touch these objects. The right-handed person would hold the spoon with the heroin in his left hand to control the lighter and the heat with his right. The bag had to have prints on it from both hands. Check.

I took the spoon and carefully placed his thumb and forefinger right where the police would look for prints on the spoon. For added measure, I made sure the middle finger was imprinted behind the forefinger too, as though he had naturally used his middle finger to support and balance the spoon.

The lighter was a little more difficult. It could not be "palmed" but rather clutched in just the fingers. The thumb had to strike and slip the flint just right. I did a couple of hand-over-hand strokes until I was sure the lighter was properly imprinted. Then I set both the spoon and the lighter on the table in front of the bastard. He was moaning softly, so I had to hurry. An overdose of heroin could take a few minutes, or it could take a little longer depending on his body weight. I had to guess since his bloated midsection looked like a dead man's weight and I wasn't about to ask him how fat he had gotten in the last twelve years.

I crossed his loose right arm over his body, and again, in hand-over-hand motion I coerced his thumb onto the plunger of the needle and placed the needle's body between his forefinger and middle finger. Then all three fingers together cradled the body of the needle to imprint it so that it would look like he had touched it prior to moving it into position to inject himself. I removed the needle at this point and dropped it on the table with everything else in a haphazard way with the point facing left. It had to look natural, but it also had to look like he was getting his buzz on just as he removed the needle.

The other end of the hose was all that was left. Hand-over-hand again, I had him clutch the opposite end of the hose, pull and squeeze. The fingerprints should look smeared and stretched when the cops dusted for them. I released the hose from his arm to let the poison completely take over. Then I made sure he palmed the hose a couple of times for good measure before untying him.

I let the hose drop where it may, under his arm where he supposedly injected himself. Pushing the chair into the table, I paused to listen for breathing. He was struggling but could not move. I took off the rag with chloroform so that it would leave his lungs before anyone could find him. I used another rag with the chemical to remove traces of chloroform so that it could not be found on is lips or facial skin later.

I sat and watched for a second, scared, but resolved. As he began frothing at the mouth, and seizing, I went looking for the kids' things I claimed to have come for. I got them, checked on the scene one last time, and walked toward the door.

A wave of peace washed over me. I felt utter relief, as though the burden of the last twenty years had been lifted. It was gone. HE was gone. I knew it might not last. I knew that I would be looking over my shoulder the rest of my days, but it would not be because of this monster.

I also knew that the kids would forgive me, if it came to that. They knew after years of having the courts force him on them that they were free too. I knew they would miss him because he was the only father they had, but they would be free, and that was the important thing. He could not lie to them, steal from them, beg off them or torture them.

As I opened the door, I called out "Goodbye!" to the corpse in the kitchen chair. The neighbors needed to hear it, even if they never got involved. I locked the door and walked out.

The plane would be leaving in less than an hour. Freedom was finally realized, and peace was mine. I would enjoy it for however long I had it.

Epilogue

The day is warm and sunny. The south of France has been such a delight these past few years. I have not had such peace before. I'm relaxing under a *parapluie de soliel*, one of the many that dot the beach today. The beautiful, sparkling waves that lap the shore lull me into a hazy, dreamlike state. Across the beach, all is calm.

In the distance, I hear a hum. It is not a hum of any creature or stationary machine. It is not the hum of any of the boats that are docked nearby. I look up and glance up and down the beach. There, in the distance, to my right, is a beachcomber vehicle. It is marked *"La Police d'Antibes"*. It is headed right for me.

I'm not sure if I should pack up and run. Maybe they aren't coming for me. I panic a little bit every time this happens but is never me they are after. I've escaped suspicion and arrest for nearly a decade now, but each time "la Police" make me nervous and then roll right by.

Before I've made a hard decision to move, the vehicle is nearly on top of my spot. The well-uniformed and well-armed *gendarmes* climb out and walk toward me. I should not flinch; after all, I'm a skeleton of my former heavy self, and my hair is silvery with perfect black and hot pink streaks in it. I look nothing like the tortured, obese woman that came here all those years ago. With my favorite pair of Louis Vuitton sunglasses on, you can't even recognize any part of the former me.

The first gendarme approaches me cautiously, plodding heavily through the sand. As he gets close enough, he speaks.

"Bonjour, Madame!"

"Bonjour, Inspecteur!" I calmly and politely reply, noticing his designation on his uniform.

"Peut-etre votre prenom et nom est Laura Thompson?" queried the inspector.

I could lie about my name, but I have been expecting this day for years. So, naturally I replied truthfully.

"Oui, Monsieur! Que'st que ca vers?" I had every right to ask what this was about, since I was pretty sure what would happen next.

"Madame, Je vous voudrais venir avec nous a le station, s'il vous plait. Nous avons quelques questions pour vous."

And there it was. Come with us to the station, we have some questions for you. Please. All of France is like that. Always polite, even when they are about to arrest you and charge you for murder. Calmly, I collected my things and prepared myself for what was finally coming at last.